THE COTTONMOUTH CLUB

THE SAVANNAH TIME TRAVEL MYSTERIES
BOOK 3

SUSAN KIERNAN-LEWIS

SAN MARCO PRESS

The Cottonmouth Club. Book 3 of The Savannah Time Travel Mysteries.
Copyright © 2024 by Susan Kiernan-Lewis

All rights reserved.

Unraveling the past can change the future...if time doesn't run out for her first.

In the third installment of the exciting Savannah time travel mysteries, Georgia Belle navigates speakeasies, flapper fashion, and a world without modern technology, all while attempting to solve a murder that has remained a mystery for a century. When she uncovers a secret Savannah society, the connections to the famous murder--and others--are undeniable. But the deeper she delves, the higher the stakes become—especially with what is happening unbeknownst to her in her personal life back in 2023. "The Cottonmouth Club" is a riveting blend of historical detail, thrilling mystery, and poignant family drama. This is a clean read with little graphic violence.

∽

Books by Susan Kiernan-Lewis
The Maggie Newberry Mysteries
Murder in the South of France
Murder à la Carte
Murder in Provence
Murder in Paris
Murder in Aix
Murder in Nice

Murder in the Latin Quarter
Murder in the Abbey
Murder in the Bistro
Murder in Cannes
Murder in Grenoble
Murder in the Vineyard
Murder in Arles
Murder in Marseille
Murder in St-Rémy
Murder à la Mode
Murder in Avignon
Murder in the Lavender
Murder in Mont St-Michel
Murder in the Village
Murder in St-Tropez
Murder in Grasse
Murder in Monaco
Murder in the Villa
Murder in Montmartre
Murder in Toulouse
A Provençal Christmas: A Short Story
A Thanksgiving in Provence
Laurent's Kitchen

The Claire Baskerville Mysteries
Déjà Dead
Death by Cliché
Dying to be French
Ménage à Murder
Killing it in Paris
Murder Flambé
Deadly Faux Pas
Toujours Dead

Murder in the Christmas Market
Deadly Adieu
Murdering Madeleine
Murder Carte Blanche
Death à la Drumstick
Murder Mon Amour

The Savannah Time Travel Mysteries
Killing Time in Georgia
Scarlett Must Die
The Cottonmouth Club

The Stranded in Provence Mysteries
Parlez-Vous Murder?
Crime and Croissants
Accent on Murder
A Bad Éclair Day
Croak, Monsieur!
Death du Jour
Murder Très Gauche
Wined and Died
Murder, Voila!
A French Country Christmas
Fromage to Eternity
Crepe Expectations

The Irish End Games
Free Falling
Going Gone
Heading Home
Blind Sided
Rising Tides
Cold Comfort

Never Never
Wit's End
Dead On
White Out
Black Out
End Game

The Mia Kazmaroff Mysteries
Reckless
Shameless
Breathless
Heartless
Clueless
Ruthless

Ella Out of Time
Swept Away
Carried Away
Stolen Away

1

"So, explain to me again," Mary said, lifting the teacup to her lips. "It just rolls around on its own and cleans your floor?"

I reached for an iced cookie, enjoying the sunlight on my face. It was a perfect early fall day in Savannah, made more perfect by having tea in Mary's glorious, southern-facing garden which was awash with the vibrant hues of blooming azaleas and camelias, their deep reds and pinks a striking contrast against the verdant greenery. The air was sweet with the scent of gardenias and magnolias.

From where I sat in my wicker chair, I could see the butterflies as they flitted from flower to flower. Bees buzzed lazily among the blooms, their industrious hum a contrast to the sluggish heat of the southern summer.

"Even I'm sort of amazed by it," I admitted. "And it's been around for years."

"You have an automated vacuum cleaner, but you still don't have a cure for cancer in 2024?" she asked.

I poured myself more tea and handed a half cookie to

Libby, my rescue mutt—although that phrase hadn't been coined yet.

"Well, they invented the floor robot at the same time they're working on the cancer cure," I said.

"I suppose it was easier to invent a robot vacuum cleaner than save millions of lives."

Mary shook her head, her dark curls shaking as she did. She was an attractive woman with soulful eyes that really held you when she looked at you. I should know since nine years from now I will do a portrait of her in oil that I'll then find in an old antique shop a hundred years from now.

"Having said that," Mary said, squinting at the double French doors off the garden that led into her townhouse, "if you do go back again, I wouldn't mind seeing one for myself. It runs on electricity, I suppose?"

"Batteries," I said. "But it charges with electricity."

It had been six months since I'd told Mary the truth of who I was and after a bit of a rough patch, she quickly adapted to the idea of her best friend as a time traveler. Now, after exhausting most of my Kindle library and downloads of Netflix videos, she was regularly grilling me for various items she might want to see for herself the next time I went back to 2024.

It sounds so casual when I phrase it like that but the actual fact of my being able to travel between two centuries was, as you might imagine, literally earth shattering when it first happened to me. And like so many life-altering events, it was a total accident. I'd left my life in 2023 Savannah and transported back to the nineteen twenties where I met Mary. And then I fell in love with a very sexy, very traditional police detective named Sam Bohannon.

"Seen Sam recently?" Mary asked, as if she could read my mind.

She asked the question offhandedly as she poured herself a cup of tea, the steam rising in gentle curls and mingling with the fragrant air.

"Not since the last time you asked," I said, pretending to focus on how cute Libby looked chasing the garden butterflies.

When I made my first appearance in 1923, Sam very quickly made his intentions known and began to court me, although at the time I wasn't sure exactly how I felt. When it became clear he wanted to marry me—things tend to move more rapidly back in these days—I confess that I acted less than honorably.

By that I mean I accepted his marriage proposal.

And then left to go back to my own time.

In my defense, I had a lot going on back in 2023—not the least of which was a job, a mother, and an apartment. But in truth, I'd been badly conflicted about what to do with Sam and so I took the easy way out. When I came back a few weeks later, he reacted with hurt and aggrieved feelings. Since then, we've made amends of sorts, but Mary is of the firm belief that I have permanently blotted my copybook with him. I have to admit one of Sam's big attractions for me was his old-world southern gentleman style. Unfortunately, as an *authentic* old-world southern gentleman, he was much less enthralled with me and my way-too-modern ways. I try very hard not to put my foot in my mouth when I'm visiting this timeline. But it's not easy. And sometimes the modern 2024 girl in me says things that can make a 1924 gentleman blush. Not a good approach when you're trying to win someone back.

"You should forget him, Georgia," Mary said. "I love Sam. You know I do. But he's never going to understand who you are—even if he never learns about the time traveling thing."

"I hear you," I said.

This was my standard answer to her when I didn't agree with what she was saying but didn't want to argue with her about it.

"He's not speaking to you, is he?" she asked.

"No, and can you believe that?" I said with irritation. "I literally solved his last murder case—his last *two* murder cases! I made him look like a hero to his boss. And in spite of that, he avoids me!"

"Did you ever think it's *because* of you winning those cases for him that he avoids you?" Mary asked, arching an eyebrow knowingly.

"Well, that just makes no sense at all."

"On the other hand, how is your Mr. O'Connell?"

I blushed at her word choice. Jim O'Connell was a private detective with whom I'd worked a case with recently. He's tall and capable and very handsome in every sense of the word.

"You know very well he's not *my* Mr. O'Connell," I said.

"Not for lack of trying on his part."

"Don't be ridiculous. I'm sure Jim has hundreds of women hanging all over him."

"Lovely image, my dear. But it doesn't address the question of the two of you."

"There is no *two of us*. I like Jim. He's great. He literally saved my life last year."

"But he's not Sam."

"I can't help how I feel," I said in frustration. "A famous filmmaker from my time has this great line that 'the heart wants what it wants.'"

"That is a good line," Mary said, nodding. "But it sounds like an excuse for wanting the wrong thing."

I was a little amazed at how on-the-nose Mary could be. Even so, there was no way I believed her view pertained to me. There was nothing wrong or inappropriate about two unmarried consenting adults wanting each other. Even if that wanting was currently a little one-sided. That situation could be fixed. Sam had wanted me desperately at one time. He'd asked me to marry him, for heaven's sakes! I was sure we could get back there again if he would just give me another chance.

"And does this torch you're carrying for Sam mean you've decided to stay in 1924?" Mary asked.

That was a fair point since the whole reason Sam and I fell apart in the first place was because I didn't feel I could commit to him or to living a hundred years in the past. I still couldn't make that commitment, but my heart didn't want to hear that. I missed him. I'd never met anyone like him. Certainly not in my own time. On some sleepless nights, I even convinced myself I could get Sam to travel with me to 2024. Although how I'd do that, is anybody's guess. I didn't fully comprehend how I did it myself.

"And what about the dangers of your time traveling?" Mary asked, munching a cookie and squinting at me in the sun.

There she went, making another stellar point just when I thought I had all the tricky details ironed out. The fact was, time traveling took it out of me. And by that, I mean it prematurely aged me. I'd done it three times in three weeks last year and later when I went to my doctor in 2023 for an answer to why I was feeling so tired lately, he did a series of tests that came back with baffling results. Chronologically, I was thirty years old. But biologically I was closer to forty.

The fact was, I was aging at an accelerated rate. It had to be the time traveling.

"I think I've figured that little mystery out," I said.

"Oh?"

"I believe I did an aging jump because I went back and forth so much last year between the centuries, so naturally there were physical repercussions."

Mary frowned. "Does that mean you're not going back to 2024?"

"Not any time soon."

"I'm glad to hear it."

She smoothed out the wrinkles in her linen shirt dress and then held out a piece of cookie to Libby. For all the complaining she'd done when I first rescued the dog, I have to say Mary is possibly even crazier about the pup than I am.

"I guess I'll just have to wait a little longer for my robot vacuum cleaner," she said.

2

I live in a two-hundred-year-old townhouse on East Perry Street, not far from Mary's place and two blocks from the famous Colonial Park Cemetery. I bought the townhouse with ill-gotten gains because for a brief time I'd needed a place to live other than Mary's. Now since that time was past, I had been tempted to sell the townhouse and move back in with Mary.

Frankly, it is a little lonely, Libby notwithstanding. In the end, I decided to hang onto the house, I think in part because I knew how much it cost in 2024. I can barely afford to walk across the street from this townhome in my own time, let alone live in it. So, I was enjoying owning it. Even though I had almost no furniture, and it was way too big for just me and one small dog.

The other problem of living here alone was the fact that since I have no staff, and there was no such thing as convenience foods back in 1924, I was basically eating a loaf of bread with cheese and apples for most of my meals. Or eating at the local diner. And trust me, if it looks weird to eat alone back in 2024, it is practically certifiable to do it in 1924.

People stare and whisper when a woman comes into a restaurant alone. I'm not sure I wouldn't rather go hungry.

Back in my shabby little block apartment in 2024 I often whip up an Instagram recipe or get my crockpot going on the weekend. But here, not only are the ingredients for meals much harder to come by, but the kitchen appliances are prehistoric. Mixing bowls, eggbeaters and a toaster are about the full range available to me, which tends to short-circuit pretty much any culinary endeavor on my part. I like to cook but I'm less excited about the prospect of having to *make* the dough before cutting out my spaghetti noodles. It's true that everything back in this time tastes amazing. But it also takes forever to prepare.

This morning, I risked the toaster malfunctioning so I could start my day with buttered toast. I made a mental note to bring some Nutella back with me next time I visited my own time. I do have a jar of homemade preserves that I got here from a market over the weekend that is so good it literally brings tears to my eyes.

After breakfast, I dressed and took Libby across the street to a very pretty little pocket park and gave her a full ten minutes to sniff the grass before putting her back in the townhouse so I could head downtown.

While I greatly appreciated Mary's words of advice when it came to Sam, I also knew that she didn't know the look I'd seen in his eye many times since we'd broken up that made me believe it wasn't over between us.

Horse-drawn carriages clattered slowly down the cobblestone road next to me, their iron-shod hooves echoing between the moss-draped oaks that lined the street. My plan to win Sam back was simple. I would wear him down with daily intrusions. I would make him realize I wasn't running off again. I would make him believe that he could trust me. I knew he didn't answer his own phone at work, and I couldn't tie up the main police line by calling him nonstop. But I could pop into the police department and sit in the waiting room until he had a moment to see me. At any rate, I thought my best chance to win him back would be in person. In the process, I would impress him with how patient and accommodating I could be. This was especially important since one of the things Sam didn't care for was my impulsiveness. This plan, I decided, was a great way to show him how tenacious yet self-possessed I could be.

As I walked down Oglethorpe Street toward the police station, I spotted a familiar form ahead of me on the sidewalk leaning on a streetlamp. I glanced at my watch. It was just a bit after ten in the morning. Jim O'Connell liked his night life so to see him before noon was an oddity to say the least. There was a distinct possibility he hadn't been to bed yet.

Or at least not his own bed.

I smiled as I approached him.

"Waiting for me?" I asked as he gave me a nod of greeting.

"Thought we could walk together," he said, "if we're going in the same direction. And I have a proposition to make to you."

Jim cocked his head and shook his hair out of his eyes. He wears it longer than most men do in this time, but it suits him. On top of that, he has a crooked grin that makes me blush just to see it.

"Why, Mr. O'Connell," I said with a coy smile. "Whatever do you mean?"

"If that's your southern belle act," he said with a grin, "it needs work."

"Hit me," I said.

He frowned in confusion.

"I mean," I said, "kindly tell me what proposition you have in mind."

"It's a job," he said as he fell into step beside me. "I'm investigating a possible embezzlement for a new client. Trace paperwork and that sort of thing. I could use a female operative to interview the employees. It's not dangerous and it pays well."

I certainly didn't need the money these days, but I didn't want to say that to Jim. He was always curious about how I was living and by what means. I should really make something up to tell him, but so far, I hadn't had the time to come up with anything believable.

"Sounds interesting," I said. "But I think I'll pass. I'm pretty busy these days."

He snorted.

"If by *busy* you mean hounding the city's number one police detective, you might want to save your effort."

"How dare you!" I said, suddenly flustered.

Had he talked to Mary? Unlikely. They were only acquainted through me. I don't know how he realized my plan. Had I said something to him? I mean, he *is* a private investigator. But it was just too annoying! It's one thing to have a plan as to how to get your beau back but it's another thing entirely to be seen as desperate. Jim held up his hands as if to fend me off.

"It's just an observation," he said, "which is after all the keystone of what I do for a living."

"I don't know where you got that idea," I said, feeling my ears burn with embarrassment. "I have no intention of *hounding* anyone."

"Oh? So, you don't care that your boyfriend was just seen

along with three other officers in a police car heading south on Oglethorpe?"

"He's not my boyfriend," I said grumpily.

But the news spoiled my mood. As disappointed as I was that Sam wasn't available to see me this morning, I hated worse that Jim could predict that the police station was where I was headed. I stopped walking, needing a moment to gather my thoughts.

"Sorry to reroute your plans for the day," Jim said.

"Not at all," I said loftily, as my mind raced for some way to wipe that smug look off his face. "As a matter of fact, I was thinking of checking out that new jazz place that opened on Barnard Street."

He frowned. "At ten in the morning?"

"I'm a big fan of jazz music."

"You're not talking about The Cottonmouth Club, are you?"

"Yes, that's it," I said. "Do you know it?"

I was feeling better now that he seemed so unhappy at the idea of my going there.

"I know it's a speakeasy," he said firmly.

"As I understand it, some of the best music is found in speakeasies," I said.

"I presume you've heard of Prohibition?" he said crossing his arms.

"Don't worry about it," I said. "As you say, it's too early to go anyway."

"Any time is the wrong time," he said. "They're drinking illegal booze in there, Georgia."

"Heavens," I said in mock horror. "You shock me, Mr. O'Connell. So, I don't suppose *you* would go there?"

"Absolutely not."

I could tell by the way he said it that he truly believed

that was the end of the discussion. It would never occur to him that I might decide to get dressed up tonight and go alone. It's a shame, too. Sam wasn't the only man in this timeline who was adorably chauvinistic.

Honestly, it's like none of them have ever even heard of women's liberation.

3

After leaving Jim, I continued on to the downtown district and did a little grocery shopping and then had lunch at The Rusty Spoon diner in the middle of town. I knew for a fact that Sam often ate at the diner, but I didn't see him today. Then I walked back home with my bag of groceries and did what I suppose most women of comfortable means did back in the twenties. I took a nap and read a book and tossed the ball with Libby in the back garden and then spent no less than two hours getting ready for tonight.

I'd gone on a shopping spree a few weeks earlier, so I had a couple of very nice frocks to choose from instead of my usual ragtag selection of largely unacceptable 2024 clothing. I'd long figured out that the shoes in this timeline didn't do my feet any favors, so I wore very pretty strappy high heels that I'd brought with me from DSW. Nobody had ever noticed them at least enough to comment on them and they were way more comfortable than any I'd found in 1924.

Then, after a long soaking bath—after all, I had plenty of time—I dressed in a fun little ensemble that I'd found in a vintage consignment shop back in my own time. It was a beaded flapper dress that hit just above the knee that I finished off with a cloche hat and fingerless silk gloves that came up to my elbow. I felt like I was going to a costume party but of course I was *au courante* for 1924.

I hated leaving Libby alone for the evening and in fact I nearly ran her down to Mary's so she wouldn't be alone, but I didn't want to have to answer any questions about where I was going tonight. Instead, I put on some music from my cellphone—I was able to play music on it but that was about it—and set it in the living room to keep the little dear company. If anybody were to hear it, I'd have way too many questions to answer over what it was, how it played music and where I got it, but I didn't anticipate any callers in the evening.

After that, I called for a hired car and stepped outside onto my porch to wait. I didn't plan on staying late at the night club. I figured that people liked to drink at all hours, so I only waited for it to get dark. I instructed the driver to let me out a block from the club and kept to the shadows as I made my way to the speakeasy in case I ran into anyone wanting to rob me. Or worse.

Like most establishments of its kind, The Cottonmouth Club was tucked away in a dimly lit alley, its unmarked entrance making it as discreet as possible. If you knew, you knew. It's what made it half the fun, the fact that it was forbidden. That and the titillating but all-too-real possibility of a police raid.

I stepped cautiously inside through the clandestine entrance, the heavy door closing with a muted thud behind me. The transition was immediate and disorienting as I stepped from a shadowed back alley of Savannah into the pulsing heart of The Cottonmouth Club. The band was playing with a wild energy, the drums beating like a racing heart while the saxophone wailed. Inside, the walls were draped in deep red velvet curtains, creating a sense of intimacy and secrecy.

The only sources of light were candles scattered throughout the room, casting dancing shadows on the faces of the patrons. As soon I entered the place I detected the aroma of cigarette smoke and perfume. Beneath it all, a hint of forbidden excitement lingered in the air which was heavy with the sweet and smoky scent of cigars, mingled with musky perfume and the sharp tang of bootleg liquor.

I heard the sound of glasses clinking as I entered, punctuated by the hushed mixture of whispers and muted laughter.

Most speakeasies were dimly lit with flickering lighting with décor consisting of walls lined with outdated posters, giving them a dingy and secretive atmosphere. The Cottonmouth Club was different. It seemed to exude a sense of clandestine luxury. The clientele was different too. Everywhere I looked was a veritable tableau of the city's elite: ingenues in beaded flapper dresses and feathered headbands laughing too loudly with politicians whose vested interests were always as hidden as the establishment itself. Wealthy tycoons, their pocket watches glinting, debating business over brandy and cards, contentedly ignoring the world beyond the club's walls.

A few couples were dancing on a small floor, perfectly embodying the spirit of the Jazz Age.

I'd heard so much about The Cottonmouth Club—not to be confused with the Cotton Club in New York which was for black patrons only. The Cottonmouth Club was segregated as nearly everything in the South was at this time. But it's main difference from other speakeasies was how elegant and refined it was.

Although of course still totally illegal.

Waiters wove through the crowd with trays of illicit cocktails: martinis, sidecars, and mint juleps prepared with a wide assortment of bootlegged spirits. At the bar, a bartender with slicked-back hair and a knowing smirk mixed drinks with an air of showmanship. I looked around and saw private booths tucked away, along with doors that no doubt led to hidden rooms—all accessible to those needing privacy for whatever backdoor affair or dirty deals needed concealment.

I immediately felt many sets of eyes upon me as I moved deeper into the speakeasy, the vibrant energy of the Cottonmouth Club seeming to wrap around me like a seductive embrace from a world thriving in the shadows of Prohibition.

The first person I saw that really stuck out to me was a mousey young woman with nondescript looks but wearing million-dollar clothes. She had on the same sort of flapper dress that I and every other woman in the place was wearing, but she wore a headband outlined in pearls with a matching beaded clutch purse and of course the *de rigeur* long pearl necklace—a default flapper accessory. She sat in a deep chair with a book in her hands, but I could tell she wasn't really reading. It was so dark in here, I couldn't imagine how reading would even be possible. Beside her sat someone who, by rights, should have caught my attention first.

This creature was the epitome of glamour. She had flashing dark eyes accentuated by thick lashes and delicately arched brows. Her hair was bobbed in the fashionable short style of the flapper and shone like raven silk. Her full lips, stained a vivid shade of crimson, were wrapped seductively around a long white cigarette holder inlaid with mother-of-pearl. Whoever she was, she must be famous. Nobody this gorgeous just walked in off the street. She was movie star material if ever I saw it. I was to find out exactly who she was within the next few seconds when the waitress came to her and breathlessly requested her autograph for the owner of the speakeasy.

"Miss Latour," the waitress gushed. "If you could sign the menu for the boss? I've seen all your movies."

The movie star looked over the waitress's shoulder and smiled at a tall bald man standing at the bar. She wrote her name with a flourish on the proffered menu card, and then flicked her fingers as if to shoo the waitress away. The waitress murmured a hurried, "Thank you, Miss Latour," and turned to bring the autograph to the bar.

Celeste Latour. Even I knew who she was, though her fame hadn't extended to my own time in 2024. She wasn't a Vivian Leigh level of famous, but she was a pretty big deal even so. Beside Latour stood a man with a singular expression on his face. I'd seen that look before on YouTube videos of the security hired to handle the crowds around Taylor Swift. This fellow was wide as a barn door and nearly as tall. His beefy arms strained the seams of his sleeveless undershirt, and I could see tattoos vivid against weathered skin. He was so obviously a bodyguard that my eyes moved on once I'd sussed him. I looked around until I saw the man sitting on the other side of the star who was most likely her husband.

This man was definitely not from Savannah. Not that we don't have good-looking men in Savannah. But he looked continental but with American style. He had a dimple in his chin and blue eyes. Also, he was constantly smiling which

I've noticed that most normal people in the nineteen twenties don't do. He wore a double-breasted jacket, a pressed shirt and French cuffs. I could see gold glinting from his wrist every time he used his hand—obviously an expensive gold watch. I don't know when Philippe Patek or Rolex came into fashion, but if they were a thing, then he was probably wearing one of them. Oddly, although he sat right next to Celeste Latour, not once did she look at him as she sipped her drink or waved to various people in the crowd.

Unhappy marriage, I decided as I watched him get up without a word and make his way to the bar. Curious, I followed him. Another man standing at the bar was watching him come.

"Is she giving you a hard time?" the man at the bar asked him.

The possible husband snorted and gave his drink order to the bartender.

"Don't worry," the other man said. "She's just got a lot on her mind with this new script."

The man I assumed was Latour's husband turned and glared at the other man.

"Are you seriously trying to tell me how to handle my own wife?" he said indignantly. "I don't need your advice, Gerald."

"Yeah, sure, Don, don't get hot under the collar," Gerald said.

Gerald wasn't dressed quite as expensively as Don, but he wasn't embarrassing anyone either. He too wore a double-breasted jacket with pin-striped slacks, although I must say I think I could smell his eau de toilette from where I was standing. Just then someone jostled me, and I lost my spot at the bar. I was intrigued though, so I maneuvered myself to the other side of Gerald. I can't help my natural curiosity about these things. When I see tension happening between people, I'm automatically fascinated. These two guys knew each other, maybe needed each other. But they definitely didn't like each other.

"If that's how you feel, Don," Gerald was saying, "why not just walk away?"

Don gave him a scorching look.

"And lose everything? Great advice, Gerry. Is that the kind of advice you've been giving Celeste? A lot of things are making sense now. No wonder she stopped getting decent scripts."

"Now, now," Gerald said. "I'm just telling you, if you really want out, you need to get up the nerve and just go."

Don dismissed him with an irritated wave of his hand and signaled to the bartender for another drink. Just then I felt someone caress my hip and I turned to see a greasy young man with hair sticking out of his head, staring drunkenly at my mouth.

"Do you mind?" I said slapping his hand away.

"I don't if you don't," he slurred.

I gave him my most disgusted look which seemed to dissuade him from any further contact, then turned back to the two men at the bar. However, they'd both moved on. That was annoying. I found it so fascinating to hear the inner workings of a celebrity couple—especially one not of my own time. It was very clear that old Donny boy was wanting out of the marriage with his famous wife but that annoying prenup was in the way. I find it so interesting the sorts of things one overhears after people have had a few drinks and don't seem to care if anyone hears them.

Little did I know how crucial this brief and fortuitous spate of eavesdropping would become to me later.

4

As I was trying to decide whether to leave or order a drink, I noticed the movie star Celeste Latour get up and head in the direction of the ladies' room. Her bodyguard dutifully walked behind her, glancing left and right as if ready to ward off anyone intending her harm. On impulse, I followed her.

The ladies' room at The Cottonmouth Club was tucked discreetly down a side hallway past a set of heavy velvet draperies. Stepping inside, the scent of lavender hung in the air. Dim gas lamps cast a flattering glow over a bank of pale porcelain fixtures. Behind an etched mirror, candles flickered beside golden combs and brushes that were laid out beside ribbons and tortoise hair pins. Plush velvet chaise lounges provided convenient places ladies could stop to freshen their makeup. Music and lively conversation floated distantly from the main room, making the ladies' lounge feel like a hidden oasis of tranquility. The atmosphere was one of sophistication, luxury and discretion befitting the well-heeled clientele. All the comforts of wealth were on display for ladies to preen in private.

In the center of the room by the mirror stood a middle-aged black woman as if at attention. She wore a black dress and a small starched white pinafore over it. Her hair was caught in a neat bun at the nape of her neck, and she wore white gloves. I caught her eye and she smiled but her attention quickly snapped back to her famous visitor.

I wasn't surprised to see Celeste Latour go straight for the vanity table in front of the mirror. She sat and immediately scrutinized her appearance in the mirror. I have to say, Celeste Latour was still turning heads at forty-five. Her dark hair was carefully coiffed in soft curls that framed her face attractively. Her makeup had been applied expertly to diminish the passage of time on her maturing complexion —until you got up close. Then she looked every moment of her forty-odd years. I suppose glaring set lights are not kind to a skin that doesn't have the benefit of Vitamin C or Retinol.

Plus, I know for a fact that happiness weighs in when it comes to beauty. And Celeste Latour did not look happy. She might exude all the sensuality and sophistication there was, she could stare down at you from a hundred cinema posters. But unhappiness took its toll. And usually, it took it right in the face.

I edged over to her.

"Hello, there," I said to her, smiling. "Welcome to Savannah. Are you here long?"

"Ugh," she said, blotting her lips with a tissue and not looking at me. "Am I not to have a single moment to myself even in the toilet?"

I was a little surprised that she called this restroom a toilet. It seemed a little low class to me. But I suppose when you're irritated, it's not easy to remember what role you're supposed to be playing.

"I'm not asking for your autograph," I said, my face reddening in spite of myself.

The restroom attendant was hearing this conversation and while I imagined she'd heard worse, I was still embarrassed.

"Millie! Where are you?" Celeste turned back to me. "Look, my girl can get you a picture. Now, do you mind?"

I was seconds from repeating to this arrogant cow that I didn't want her damn autograph when she knocked over a bottle of cologne on the table, spilling its contents everywhere. Instantly the attendant was there with a rag, mopping up the liquid.

"You can do that when I'm gone!" Latour said to her sharply.

"Ma'am?" the attendant said in confusion.

I'd be confused too. What was the harm in cleaning up the mess that Celeste Latour had made?

"I see you watching me," Latour said to the black woman, grabbing her hand to forcibly stop her from cleaning the counter.

The attendant looked around in bewilderment and fear.

"Stop that," I said to Latour. "She's only doing her job."

Behind me I could feel two or three women who'd come in with me quickly turn to leave.

"How dare you?" Latour said to me, standing up from her cushioned chair. "Do not pretend to lecture me on how to treat servants."

"She's not a servant," I said, knowing I should probably shut up and let this blow over but unable to stop myself.

Celeste gave her no doubt very expensive sequined flapper dress an irritated jerk to straighten out the creases from having been seated, and then walked to the tip jar on the table and deliberately knocked it over, spilling the pennies and dimes onto the floor.

"Well, she takes whatever tips her betters throw at her," she said. "So I guess you're right. She's even less than a servant."

I was so shocked that I just stood there for a moment with my mouth open before getting on my knees to pick up the coins.

"Oh, no, Miss!" the attendant said. "You shouldn't do that."

"I'm sorry," I said, my eyes now smarting with unshed tears. "I made it worse. I should have kept my mouth shut."

Except how could I? People who take advantage of their position and wealth to make other people feel bad are the worst kind of people. But I'd certainly made the situation worse. I secretly slipped a twenty-dollar bill into the tip jar. I would've left more but I didn't know if the attendant's employer demanded to see tips at the end of the night—certain restaurant managers do back in 2024. If she were found with a hundred-dollar bill, she might even be arrested for theft.

Knowing the twenty didn't make up for Latour's rudeness, I murmured my apologies to the attendant and made my way out of the ladies room, still seething.

I had no sooner set foot into the hallway when all hell broke loose.

It began with an ungodly pounding on the front door that seemed to reverberate throughout the entire night club. Conversation faltered and then stopped as startled faces turned towards the sound. Another series of staccato booms shook the heavy wood, sending ripples through the room.

The band halted mid-song.

"It's the cops!" someone screamed, and chaos erupted as patrons scrambled for exits.

Glasses hit the floor. Chairs screeched across the tile. The front door burst open with a loud crack, and at least eight uniformed police swarmed inside, nightsticks aloft.

"Raid! Everybody freeze!" a gruff voice bellowed.

People froze mid-flight, panicked eyes darting everywhere for the nearest escape. In my experience, whenever normal citizens are told to freeze, they tend to do just that. It's only the ruffians and n'er-do-wells that think about ignoring orders given by authority figures. Myself, I was a bit in-between when it came to obeying orders. I'd known plenty of so-called authority figures who were nearly as bad as the villains they were supposed to be controlling. On the other hand, I knew I was also somewhere I shouldn't be.

Out of the corner of my eye I saw Celeste Latour being hustled out of the place by her bodyguard through a side door and a part of me flushed with resentment that she was managing to escape. I was nowhere near that side door and to get there, I'd have to pass by three very angry looking young policemen holding batons.

After that, things happened quickly. The police charged into the thick of the crowd and began herding us all like startled cattle.

"Line up against the wall! Hands where I can see 'em!"

Whiskey-slurred protests rose and were cut short by baton threats. As I stood, shivering in my thin dress, I watched the doors to the kitchen fly open where I glimpsed barrels of contraband ale being frantically jettisoned out the back door. The once merry and bustling speakeasy was now emptying. My heart lurched as a large policeman grabbed me by the arm.

"You're coming with us, toots," he said gruffly.

I wanted to protest but found my throat dry and no words would come. He dragged me outside where a further chaotic scene awaited. A mob had gathered to jeer at the shame-faced partygoers who were emerging from the speakeasy, some in handcuffs. I locked eyes with a man I'd seen at the bar. I'm sure he was a prosperous businessman who was now going to be shamed before the world. Or maybe not. Maybe he'd just pay someone off and slip away as if tonight had never happened.

The paddy wagon sat parked and waiting, its metal interior already steaming from the packed, sweating bodies inside. The acrid stench of fear flooded my nostrils as I was shoved onboard. Every seat was already crowded. I stood clutching a strap for balance as more unlucky souls were forced on board behind me. One man wept openly, his expensive suit in tatters. As the wagon lurched into motion, I felt sick to my stomach.

Here we go, I thought miserably as the wagon's miserable cargo rocked back and forth, all dignity lost, riding as criminals all, toward an uncertain fate.

5

I'd have to say that night was one of the most unpleasant of my life.

Not that the company was so bad. Instead of prostitutes, drug addicts and petty thieves, I was surrounded by the well-heeled, well-dressed elite, although most of them were in tears. I started up a conversation with one woman, but her husband made her stop when it became clear that I'd been at The Cottonmouth Club without an escort. I suppose he assumed I must be a prostitute.

Once out of the paddy wagon, we were herded en masse to a series of interconnected jail cells with cold metal benches and not even the proverbial toilet you always see in convict movies. Not that anyone with me wouldn't rather cut their own throat than use a toilet with so many onlookers. I'd found a corner on a bench although it was impossible to sleep. Even so, the night went fairly quickly. One by one, people were led away, bailed out by relatives, until I was left with only about a handful of people. My new friend and her husband were practically the first ones released and the way the bailiff escorted them out, he was practically apologizing for the inconvenience, I suppose they must be important, or at least the husband.

I checked my purse to see if I had enough to bribe the bailiff, but I only had a five. It might make a decent tip but nothing more. And anyway, I wasn't in the tipping mood.

"Georgia Belle," a familiar voice intoned from the hallway.

I looked up and felt the dread that I'd kept at bay all night when I saw none other than my ex-fiancé Sam Bohannon standing on the other side of the bars. I'd been planning on telling him how this was all a terrible misunderstanding, but I know how he feels about lying and honestly, I was tired, and I looked like hell. I just didn't have the gumption at the moment to stick the lie.

I got up from the bench when he called my name and went to the door which the jailer was busy opening. I decided making any sign that I knew Sam would only embarrass him and so I refrained. Besides, Sam looked very angry.

I stepped outside and as soon as the bailiff walked on ahead, I turned to Sam.

"Thank you so much for this," I said, feeling an uncomfortable thickness in my throat.

"Don't thank me," Sam said curtly as he continued to walk.

I followed him down the same long, cold hallway that had led me to my night of shame and discomfort. We walked to the same registration window where a sergeant sat with a big book. I assumed I was now being officially processed out. Then I noticed Jim standing at the end of the hall.

Immediately I felt an unexpected release of tension, just seeing him. Tears wells up in my eyes, but I quickly brushed them away. Jim glanced only briefly at me before turning away to finish my processing with the sergeant. Then Sam turned on his heel and walked off without another word. I stared at his retreating back in utter astonishment. Then I ground my teeth as I felt the waves of rippling hurt and anger. What in the world did Sam have to be angry about?

I was the one who had singlehandedly helped him get his last rise in rank! Not to mention, if it weren't for me, he'd still be trying to hang an innocent man!

"Are you ready?"

I turned to see Jim who's own thunderous expression wasn't much better than Sam's.

"Thank you for this," I said.

"Don't thank me," he said gruffly, making me wonder if he and Sam were in some kind of mutual bad-tempered men's club. I followed him down the hall toward the door and outside.

"Why is everyone so cross with me?" I said to Jim's back.

He stopped abruptly and looked at me. Around us, people moved, spoke, yelled and argued. I have to say there was a peculiar smell to the place, too—a mixture of body odor and cigarette smoke mostly—and from the few poor unfortunates I saw handcuffed to chairs, a definite whiff of desperation.

"Okay," I said when Jim squared off with me, his arms crossed, as he confronted me. "I get why you're sore. You had to come down here in the middle of the night and bail me out. I'll pay you back, by the way. But what's Sam's problem? *I* was the one who spent a night in jail!"

"You don't know?" Jim said, tilting his head as if to understand me better.

I shook my head. He snorted and rubbed a hand across his face.

"It because of me," he said. "Do you remember that Sam and I used to be friends?"

"Used to be?" I said, completely mystified. "Why aren't you still friends? And why is he mad at me for that?"

"He's mad because I'm here bailing you out," he said as if explaining it to a simpleton.

I still wasn't getting his point which I'm sure was clear by the look on my face. He took me by the arm and led me none too gently out the door.

"He's jealous, Georgia," he said. "And take it from me, that's no fun."

6

The bath I took that night had to be the most luxurious self-indulgent soak I've ever had. I literally felt as if I was washing off the dust and the skin cells of the people I'd shared that jail cell with. Libby sat nearby on a cushion, so we were practically eye level. She had given me such an enthusiastic homecoming that it rather made up for Jim and Sam's petulance over my evening. I have to say it was nice being adored like this.

Getting Libby had been totally serendipitous. I hadn't been smart enough to know ahead of time how marvelous owning a dog would be. I made a mental note to get one when I went back permanently to 2024.

After Jim told me the reason Sam was so mad, all I could think of was how I might be able to use his jealousy to win him back. I have to say that, as much as I struggle with whether or not to stay in 1924 or go back to 2024, all I wanted to do when I was in jail was go home to my own apartment and feel my mother's arms around me. Now that might be understandable under the circumstances, but I wasn't sure if it was a good enough reason—now that I was free—to suffer the risks and tribulations of another time traveling episode so soon after my last one.

For all my bravado, Mary's worry about my premature aging and its connection to my time travel is one that worries me too. My own theory for why it was happening was sketchy. But since there was nothing on the Internet to suggest anything different, and I certainly couldn't ask my primary physician for his thoughts, I decided to believe it was due to the physical demands of traversing different time periods which must inevitably put an immense stress on my body and cells. It made sense that the experience would accelerate the aging process at a cellular level.

Another possibility was something I did find on the Internet in a Science Fiction chat room that had to do with exposure to temporal radiation. Basically, moving through the time stream subjects me to unknown forms of radiation or energy that damage my cells and exceeds the limits that my body can handle. I'm sure there are a million other possible reasons, but I have no clue as to what they are. All I know is that the more I travel between the centuries, the faster I age.

A part of me thinks it's ridiculous to even consider staying in 1924. For what possible reason would I? I have a mother in 2024. It's the time I was born into. And frankly the prospect of Sam ever coming around to wanting to date me again was starting to look more and more bleak. In any case, while I hated going back so soon—especially because of the whole premature aging thing—I did have a few things to attend to back in 2024. I needed to empty out my bank account and pay for the next three months on my apartment lease so that I'd at least have it when I decided to come back for good. I'd thought about using some of the money I had made here due to my good fortune at the horse tracks. I was rolling in dough as they say in 1924. But I feared asking the Wells Fargo branch in my 2024 neighborhood to handle currency circa 1915 might raise eyebrows.

Also, I wanted to renew my driver's license, check in with my mom and catch up with Jazz, my best buddy and workmate back in 2024. I'm sure Jazz was wondering what had happened to me. I pretty much fell off the map when I walked away from the Dispatch department of the Savannah Police Department last fall. Truth be told, they were going to fire me anyway because, what with the time traveling, I'd started missing a lot of days.

As I felt my bath water cool, I felt for the towel on the floor by the tub. I thought about telling Mary that I was going to make a quick trip back to my own time, but I knew she'd give me grief about it. I glanced at Libby. If I made it super quick—if I was able to do it all in a day—I wouldn't need to leave Libby with Mary which meant I could leave without Mary knowing.

Satisfied with this plan, I toweled off and then went to pack a few things for my trip.

7

Sam watched from his office window as Jim stopped on the street to help Georgia into his car. Georgia laughed and said something to him which made Jim shake his head. But Sam wasn't fooled by the man's nonchalance. Jim was in love with her. A blind man could see it.

He felt his hands curl into fists by his side as his muscles quivered in anger. Just watching the two of them sent a jolt of jealousy bubbling through him that made him grip the window frame until his knuckles blanched.

What had he expected? That other men wouldn't find her attractive? Had he hoped her strangeness—to the point of near eccentricity!—and her relentless independence would scare off any other suitors? He rubbed his temple and turned away from the view. He hated feeling this way. He didn't want her. That much he knew.

But he didn't want anyone else to have her either.

"Sir?"

Sam looked up to see Patrick Murphy standing in his door.

"Yes?" Sam said, turning his attention to his desk and the piles of file folders stacked on it. "What is it?"

Murphy entered the room. Like a lot of the beat cops, he was bull-necked and wide. The perennially flushed face announced his Irish heritage. Or was that the drink? Sam wondered.

"I forgot to ask permission, sir," Murphy said, twisting his hands in front of him, "but I'm doing some moonlighting for a group needing extra security."

Sam frowned. They weren't short staffed right now, so as long as Murphy did his usual beat, it wasn't a problem.

"What group?" Sam asked.

"You know that movie star in town? Celeste Latour? Her people reached out. I already worked one night."

Sam narrowed his eyes at the big man.

"Her group wasn't at the Cottonmouth Club by any chance, were they?"

"No sir," Murphy said innocently.

Sam knew the man was lying but since he'd obviously gotten his client out before the raid happened, there was no harm done.

"So is it okay?" Murphy asked.

"How long are they in town for?"

"A week. They're doing some kind of picture promotion and then they go back to California."

Sam knew Murphy had a wife and three kids. The extra money would no doubt come in handy.

"Sure," Sam said. "But mind you keep her out of the speakeasies."

Patrick laughed.

"I'll try," he said with a grin. "But I'm not sure you know too many movie stars if you think they listen to what I say."

Sam grinned too. It felt like the first time he'd smiled in days.

"Better you than me," he said. "Life is hard enough without dealing with prima donnas."

After that, Murphy left and Sam turned back to his desk and tried to reclaim the feeling of that recent smile. But every time he did, an image of Georgia walking so close to Jim O'Connell came thundering back to him.

8

In my experience, time travel can be compared to the electrifying experience of a roller coaster ride—it's both exhilarating and disorienting. And also terrifying, of course. There's never a time I do it that I don't worry for at least a moment that I'll end up in the Cretaceous or Jurassic Age and I'm not talking about the fun Spielberg movie. But that terror aside, I do my best to focus my thoughts on where I'm going. If I can shut out all other stimuli and just zero in on what it feels like to be in the age I'm aiming for, I think it mitigates the physical discomfort of the experience. At least a bit.

I've also discovered that if I start out in my home I will somehow transport to the locale of my other home. So, leaving from my garden in 1924 tends to take me to my back patio of my apartment in 2024. I say *tends to* because it's not an exact science. Or maybe it is, and I just don't know science well enough to know how to finesse it every time.

It was midmorning when I locked Libby in the house and went to a wrought iron bench in my garden. I sat down and closed my eyes and began to focus on being back in

2024. Sometimes it took an hour to make it work, and sometimes I'd barely sat down, and I was gone. This time it was closer to the latter. Almost as soon as I sat down, I felt a sudden, intense surge of energy that seemed to buzz through every cell in my body. A dizzying array of lights and colors swirled around me, seeming to blur the lines between the physical space I was occupying and the temporal vortex I hoped to enter.

My stomach lurched exactly as it does on the precipitous drop of a roller coaster. The world outside my garden immediately began to stretch and distort, much like the scenery whipping past a roller coaster car in full descent. Even sounds—the distant twitter of birds and traffic—seemed to warp around me in a cacophony that could be likened to what you'd hear on a high-speed coaster. The usual clacks and clangs of the roller coaster track were replaced by the pulsating thrum of time being bent and folded.

For a moment, everything felt suspended, as if I was at the apex of the roller coaster's highest climb with the world hanging in a balance between past and future. Then, with a whoosh that snatched my breath away, time rushed forward, and I felt myself hurtling through the temporal tunnel.

The end always came suddenly. There was a jarring sensation, as if a roller coaster car slammed on the brakes at the end of a wild ride. Then the world gradually eased back into focus, as sounds and sights slowly normalized. The only thing still speeding was my pulse.

I looked around and saw that I was on a children's playground—not my back patio. There was nobody there, but I quickly scrambled to my feet and dusted off my clothes. I'd worn leggings and sneakers—clothes I kept hidden in the back of my closet in 1924. I was about a block from my apartment complex and after giving a silent prayer of gratitude that I'd landed in 2024—and not 56BCE—I hurried down the street to my apartment.

My apartment building is an example of a typical contemporary structure amidst an urban landscape. It's a medium-rise edifice with a facade that is a combination of reflective glass and cool, neutral-toned panels. It's not pretty, but the rent is priced accordingly. There is no landscaping near the building—landscaping costs money and is clearly unnecessary since the apartments are always full. My address is located on a street off the main drag. I pay extra to be so close to downtown. After I pay the rent for the next ninety days I'll need to decide if the extra expense of that is worth it.

As I unlocked the front door and stepped into my apartment, I found myself grateful they hadn't turned the electricity off. I wasn't sure how behind I was in paying my bill. Inside, I saw a scattering of second-class bills and flyers piled up on the floor from where they'd been deposited through the front door's mail slot. The air smelled odd to me. Nothing I could put my finger on, just that very modern neutral aroma from an HVAC system that circulates air. Even the air was different back in 1924.

The first thing I noticed after the mail was the dead begonia on the kitchen counter and the blinking microwave oven clock. There must have been a power surge or maybe a storm took the lights out at one point while I'd been gone. I immediately plugged in my cellphone to the charger in the kitchen. I bring my phone with me to the twenties for its camera capabilities and to show photos to Mary. Now, it lit up and I saw all my unread emails and text messages tumble across the screen.

I quickly clicked on a voicemail message from my mother that had come in last night.

"Hi, sweetie. Haven't seen you in a bit and was hoping we could grab lunch. I'm heading back to the hospital for a few more of those dratted routine tests. Nothing to worry about. Just like to connect with my baby girl."

I looked at my watch. It was already past twelve, so lunch was out. I really wanted to check in with her, but it looked as if she already had a busy calendar today at the hospital. I wondered what sort of tests she was having done. Her message said *routine* but last fall I'd accompanied her for a series of tests that were anything but. Thankfully, the results of those tests had all come back negative.

I got an image in my mind of little Libby sitting next to her empty food bowl, waiting for me, and that decided the question for me. I'd catch Mom next time. By then, she'd have more to tell me when we sat down to lunch. I fired off a quick text message to her saying I couldn't make it this week because I was once more going undercover and would be incommunicado on a perfectly safe exercise for the Savannah police but I'd be in touch soon.

My mother didn't know I'd lost my job last year because of my erratic attendance. I didn't tell her because I didn't want her to worry. So I made up a story for her about going undercover. She never called me at work so that wasn't a worry. I glanced at my watch. Speaking of work, I was keen to hear all the news of what was going on there, so I put a call in to Jazz. I knew she was working, and they frowned on anyone taking personal calls, but I'd leave a message and she'd get back to me when she could.

My first stop after that was the bank to write a check for my apartment rent and to take the rest of my funds out in cash for some purchases I needed to make today. Because of my knowledge of the future and which horse races in 1923 would pay off, I'd made quite a bit of money which allowed me to live comfortably in 1924. However, money was an issue in 2024. I was barely able to hang onto my apartment, and they'd already cut off the electricity twice before for nonpayment. Ugh. No one ever talks about the inconveniences of time travel.

As I hurried down the street to my local Wells Fargo branch, I found myself amazed at everything around me. Just yesterday, this street had been mud-filled with horses crapping all over it and men in handlebar mustaches strolling along twirling umbrellas past shops named *Sweet Shoppe* and *Waldo's Fantastic Emporium*.

I passed a *Five Guys* burger place, then turned right around and went in and ordered a double cheeseburger with onion rings and a chocolate shake. It's true that food back in the old days is amazing. But there are some things for which there is no replacement. When I sat down at the counter facing West Congress Street to eat it, I found myself nearly in tears of ecstasy.

After lunch, I continued my trek to the bank, passing the building where the police station in 1923 had been. It was nearly impossible for me to believe that I'd spent a night there just a day ago for having a drink in a speakeasy. I felt a wave of undefinable emotion. Thinking of that night made me think of what Jim had said about Sam being angry because he was jealous. Just the thought of that buoyed me considerably.

The more I thought of it, the more I knew I needed to get back to 1924 as soon as possible to strike while the proverbial iron was hot.

I raced through my errands, skipping the license renewal after all, but hitting a Best Buy. Then I cleaned out my fridge back at the apartment although I was sure I'd be back at the end of the month, and tossed the dead begonia in the trash. Then, after packing my backpack with a few items that I'd purchased today, I took one last look at my apartment—especially my automatic coffee maker—and prepared to go back to 1924 where I had a good man waiting for me.

Even if he didn't know it.

9

Coming back this time was weird.

It's true that each time I do it something is different but this time it was *way* different. The experience felt less like a trip on an unfettered roller coaster and more like being led down a circuitous mountain path by a sadistic tour guide. As soon as I settled down on a plastic chair on my apartment patio and closed my eyes things began to happen.

I barely had time to envision 1924—and Sam, who was usually my guiding star in these 1924-bound trips—when all of a sudden, I felt as if I was walking alone down a dark wooded path. Everything began to swirl and distort around me. I felt dizzy and disoriented, as if the ground was dropping out from under my feet. It was like the sensation of semi-lucid dreaming—being partially aware but unable to control what was happening. Shapes and colors blended together in a kaleidoscopic whirl. Trees morphed into amorphous blobs of green and brown that spun sickeningly around me.

A roaring filled my ears, like the static noise you hear

just before losing consciousness. My mind couldn't make sense of the chaos assaulting my senses. Snatches of images flashed in my head—a horseless carriage careening down the road, banners declaring votes for women, men in top hats and tails.

Everything was vibrating at a high frequency. I felt as if I was teetering on the edge of oblivion. Then, just as suddenly, the tumult ceased. I pitched forward onto my hands and knees. My mind raced to catch up as my surroundings slowly came into focus. I was supposed to be in my townhouse garden with grass and dirt under my hands and knees.

Instead, I felt a hard, gritty surface. Where had the vortex deposited me? A terror flooded me as I wondered for one mad moment if I'd been taken to a different time, but as the swirling chaos settled, I heard music and laughter and realized I was kneeling on the floor of a boisterous night club. Panic rippled through me.

I wasn't dressed properly to be seen in public for 1924. My leggings were form-fitting and left nothing to the imagination. I was wearing a midriff-baring yoga top. In fact, I could be arrested for showing so much of my body. I tried to manage my burgeoning panic and hauled myself to my feet with the help of a nearby bar stool. Jazz music blared. Smoky air hung thick as patrons all around me talked and laughed and drank. Men in pinstriped suits and women in beaded flapper dresses milled about, oblivious to me. For now.

At least I was in the nineteen-twenties. I put my hand on the bar and turned to try to get my bearings when an abrupt flash of light exploded in my face. I blinked and felt as if stardust had been blown into my face. I was back to swirling and floating with the darkness pushing at the edges of my mind. The club melted away like a dream replaced by a bad case of vertigo. Just when I was sure I would throw up, it was over. I felt grass beneath me.

I knew I was physically no longer moving but my head continued to spin for long seconds after my body had physically stopped. I opened my eyes and looked up to see the familiar treetops of my back garden swaying overhead. Somewhere in the background I heard the excited but muted yapping of Libby desperate to get out into the garden to greet me. I filled my lungs with the cool night air, grounding me back in reality.

I was home.

10

The next morning, I went to visit Mary and carefully unboxed the Roomba I'd brought back with me, mindful of her rapt gaze. I placed the sleek, disc-shaped device on the hardwood floor of her front salon.

"Are you ready for this?" I asked.

"I can't remember ever being more excited," Mary said in a reverent whisper.

With a sense of ceremony, I tapped the start button on the machine. The device beeped cheerfully, prompting a squeal of delight from Mary, whose eyes were wide with a mixture of skepticism and wonder. The little machine quickly hummed to life, gliding across the floor with grace and confidence, turning and twisting around obstacles as if it had been vacuuming Mary's living room for years. Mary clapped her hands in delight.

As I explained to Mary how the little robot used sensors to navigate and avoid falling downstairs or getting stuck under furniture, the whir of the Roomba's motor filled the room. Mary ran after the contraption, her eyes following

Roomba as it dutifully scooted under her sofa, reappeared on the other side, and continued across the room. Mary laughed out loud.

"It picked up the dust! Did you see that?!"

I grinned at Mary's reaction. Something so commonplace to me was a marvel through her eyes—an impossible combination of innovation and automation that transcended the boundaries of time. At one point, the machine stopped, and a chime sounded.

"Move Roomba to another location!" it chirped.

The scream that followed made both Mary and me snap our heads around to see Cook standing in the doorway, a tray of tea and cookies in her trembling hands and her mouth open in shock.

∽

An hour later, after assurances from us that we would put Roomba back in its box while Cook was in the house, Mary and I sat outside in her garden and enjoyed the tea Cook had nearly dropped all over the just cleaned salon floor.

"The good news is you don't look any older," Mary said over her teacup as she narrowed her eyes at me. "Maybe a few more gray hairs?"

"Ha!" I said. "No way."

The fact was, I *had* seen a few more gray hairs this time and while I hated that, I still felt as young as ever. Besides which, I'd brought back a couple cans of roots concealer with me.

"How do you feel? Did you see your mother?" she asked.

"I feel great. I didn't see her, no, because she was getting some hospital tests done. I'll see her next time. I basically went back to pay my apartment rent and get the Roomba."

"Well, in any case," Mary said. "I'm delighted with Roomy. I can't wait to take him to the upstairs bedrooms. The maids don't do near well enough on the carpets up there."

I knew that Mary hired a service to do basic housekeeping and I also knew she'd prefer not to rely on them so much.

"I'm sorry I didn't tell you I was going," I said. "But it was just a quick there and back to get a few things done that I should've handled earlier."

"In the meantime, you probably haven't heard the news," she said.

"What news?"

"About that movie star who was in town?"

"Celeste Latour?" I asked.

"That's her. Well, she was at this illegal club on Barnard Street last night when she had a heart attack and fell down dead!"

I was literally speechless. Maybe even a little dizzy at hearing this news. I instantly flashed back to that moment last night when I'd accidentally transported briefly to what I now believed to be the Cottonmouth Club. I remembered the pandemonium and chaos all around me. I guess I thought that had all just been a part of the transport experience—like a memory of the place that was locked in my brain and accessed when I started time tripping. Had I really been there? Could it have been around the time that Latour died?

"That's terrible," I said.

"All of Hollywood is in shock," she said.

I fell slightly nauseated at the thought that the woman I'd met a few days earlier—so vibrant and alive if haughty and annoying—was now gone.

"She seems awful young to be dying of a heart attack," I said. "Did anyone know she had a heart condition?"

"I don't know. The papers didn't say."

"It's just that, honestly, she looked the picture of health to me just a few days ago."

"Wait, what? You're not saying you *met* her?"

"I did. Last week. We even spoke."

"Where?"

"At the same club I guess she died in," I said.

"You went to The Cottonmouth Club?"

She covered her mouth. Her eyes were wide with shock.

"It's no big deal, Mary," I said. "Women in my time do that sort of thing all the time."

"Do they do it when it's against the law?" she asked archly.

I had to admit she had a point there.

Later, that afternoon, Libby and I headed back home. I was smack in the middle of a few renovation projects, and I'd brought back with me a battery-operated power drill, an orbital sander that ran on electricity, although I wasn't sure if the voltage I had in my place in 1924 would handle it, and a laser leveler. I was excited to start on the projects but the minute I stepped through the door, the phone rang. I disconnected Libby from her leash and hurried to answer it.

"Hello?" I said breathlessly, sure it was Sam.

"It's Jim," he said.

"Oh, hey, Jim," I said, hoping I'd sufficiently camouflaged the disappointment in my voice. "What's up?"

"Pardon?"

"How are you?" I amended.

"Fine, fine. I wanted to know if you wanted to take a walk tonight after dinner."

"A walk?"

I tried to wrack my brain. Was that a thing back in these times? A walking date?

"You know," I said. "I'm really busy. But maybe another time?"

"How about dinner tomorrow?"

I took in a breath.

"You know, that sounds lovely, Jim, but honestly, I have so much going on. Can I take a raincheck?"

"Sure," he said, the disappointment thick in his voice.

"But listen, I'm glad you called," I said, eyeing Libby who was sniffing at the boxes of the things I'd brought back from 2024. "Only now I really must go. I have some things I need to do."

"Sure," he said. "We'll...talk soon."

"Sounds good."

I hung up and walked over to where Libby was inspecting the boxes. I rubbed my hands together with absolute glee. Not only was I going to be able to do all the projects I'd come up with to update this townhouse—something I had no doubt would totally impress Sam when he saw the end result—but I had also come up with a brilliant idea of how to get him back.

I picked up Libby and twirled around the living room while she happily licked my face. In fact, the more I thought about how genius my idea was, the more I wanted to shout for the pure joy of it—or at the very least, start picking out my trousseau.

11

The next morning, I was up early. I'd brought a box of Pop Tarts back with me and those, along with some hazelnut-flavored coffee creamers for my coffee, served as my breakfast before I began on the renovations of my townhouse. I am actually not a very handy sort of person. I can hang a shelf or a few framed pictures and I can unjam a clogged garbage disposal, but for anything else I was always thankful for a landlord I could just call up.

Now that I was a legit property owner for the first time in my life, I was determined to do things on my own. To that end, I'd downloaded some do-it-yourself videos on YouTube onto my cellphone. My phone wasn't good for much in 1924, but it did function as a handy little video player—especially since the charger I used worked with the voltage back here.

I fell asleep last night watching these how-to videos—in part because they were so boring, but also because the first day after time travel is always exhausting. Now, with breakfast behind me and a quick walk with Libby to the park across the street, I was ready to begin.

With sandpaper in hand, I knelt on the hardwood floor

of the foyer and began to smooth out its rough patches. The orbital sander I'd brought back worked beautifully and didn't trip any breakers in the process for which I was grateful. One of the projects I wanted to tackle was re-doing the kitchen cabinets. I'd thought about bringing a paint sprayer from my neighborhood ACE Hardware store in 2024 but that would involve me setting up the cabinets in the back garden to spray them and then praying nobody saw what I was doing. In the end the prospect was just too nerve-racking so I opted to brush on the varnish the old-fashioned way.

But back to the foyer floor. Once I'd finished sanding the spots that needed attention, I carefully taped off the baseboard and got to work with a fresh can of white paint, meticulously painting each corner and edge of the bead board and base board. And hour later, after hanging the colorful draperies that I'd found at a quaint hardware store down the street, I stepped back to admire my handiwork. I was delighted with my efforts.

I'd also brought a box of nails that were coated with stainless steel so that they would be more durable. I was fully prepared to tell any nosy helpers or workmen that I might hire down the line that I'd bought them in Europe—if they were curious enough to ask. Meanwhile, the people who own this townhouse in 2024 should get down on their knees and thank me for the renovations I was doing. There was no doubt in my mind the improvements I was trying to make would stand for another hundred years.

∽

I had just stopped for a lunch of chicken salad with potato chips—brought back from the little deli down the street from my 2024 apartment—when there was a knock at my front door. Grumbling that this would be a great time to have someone to answer the door for me, I peeked out the side light and saw Jim standing there, his hat in his hands, looking at his feet. I frowned because I'd specifically told him last night that I wasn't able to see him today. I opened the door.

Libby ran to the door and immediately jumped up on his knees in an exuberant greeting. I hadn't yet figured out a way to train her not to do that.

"Hey, you," I said. "Just in the area?"

Jim leaned over to pet Libby, but his face quickly morphed from a neutral smile to an expression of shock. That's when I realized I was wearing skinny jeans, Converse sneakers and a sweatshirt—all of which were coated with sanding dust.

What the hell...in for a penny...

I opened the door wider.

"I'm just having lunch," I said. "You're welcome to join me."

Jim peered around as he entered the foyer.

"What in the world are you doing?" he asked.

"I'm spot sanding the floor," I said. "And I'm just about to get the kitchen cabinets ready to be varnished."

He turned to look at me in total shock.

"You're...what?" he said.

I led the way into the kitchen where I'd just finished cleaning out the cabinets and took a plate from the stack on the counter.

"It's not fancy," I said, as I quickly put together another chicken salad sandwich.

I have to say the bread during this early twentieth century time is amazing. I think it's a real shame the particular skillset didn't seem to have lasted to my own time. I added a few chips to his plate and set it on the kitchen table where he was sitting.

"Do you want iced tea?" I asked.

He looked at it and then me in confusion.

"I don't understand," he said.

"It's tea that's served cold," I said.

"No, I..." He ran a hand through his hair and then looked down at the sandwich. "Grapes and nuts?"

I couldn't not laugh. The look on his face was priceless. I guess if you never in your life thought of a chicken salad sandwich as having grapes and nuts in it, you'd look exactly the way he was looking right now. I was glad I'd decided not to add the curry. He'd probably be organizing a mob with pitchforks to run me out of town about now.

I went to the icebox and took out a pitcher of iced tea and poured him a glass, then put the sugar bowl on the table. Jim tentatively picked up his sandwich and bit into it. I wasn't too impressed. After all, Savannah practically invented eating raw oysters. How scary could a chicken salad sandwich be? I tried not to watch him, but I was curious, and then delighted to see his face register pleasure. He drank his tea, eschewing the sugar, and I fed crusts of my own sandwich to Libby under the table.

"So why are you doing all this on your own?" he asked through a mouthful of chicken salad.

"Mostly to prove that I can," I said.

I knew enough at this point not to tell him that part of my motivation was to show Sam how capable I was. Me renovating my townhouse was just another way of presenting myself to Sam as the total package. Beautiful, smart, and know my way around an electric drill. Every man's dream.

"Can I help?" Jim asked.

"Are you very handy?" I asked.

He shrugged which I took as a modest affirmative.

"I'll never say no to help," I said. "I was just going to take the cabinets down and refinish them."

"You're going to take them *down*?"

He looked at me in surprise and then up at the cabinets.

"Well, I thought it would be easier that way," I said, "to varnish them."

He frowned as he was clearly trying to imagine what that would look like. I'd thought about painting them white, but the townhouse didn't really have a very cottage-y vibe to it. It wasn't really to-the-manor-born either like Mary's. I thought the natural wood spruced up was a more natural look.

At one point while we were working in the foyer, I saw him pick up my laser leveler and I froze. I thought I'd hidden all the modern tools when he was in the kitchen washing his hands after lunch but somehow, he spotted it. When he turned the leveler on and the little laser flipped on, his eyes widened. I cleared my throat.

"You, uh, point it wherever you, uh want to know if something's level," I said, blushing darkly and wishing I'd hidden the stupid thing better.

He watched the laser beam shoot across the room. Then he set it down and repositioned it so that the laser shot up the wall.

"Incredible," he murmured.

"Yep," I said hurriedly, "those Europeans sure are clever. Anyway, I'm not sure we need that right now."

"Right."

There was no mistaking that look of confused suspicion on his face. Seeing it made me nervous. I know Jim doesn't know much about me, and he could never in a million years guess the truth about who I am. But he knew something wasn't right. And that was never a comfortable position to be in no matter what time you live in.

Soon enough though, he got busy replacing a few rotten wood slats on the front porch while I lightly sanded the kitchen cabinets. We worked together in companionable silence. I was tempted to put some music on through my laptop or cellphone. I knew I could probably explain it as some kind of newfangled European contraption like I did the laser leveler. But in the end, I wasn't keen on getting him wondering about me unless it was absolutely necessary.

The rest of the afternoon went by quickly and honestly it was a lot more fun with Jim helping. He has a very dry sense of humor and even though I know he's endured a lot of tragedy in his life—especially during the war—he was easygoing and constantly joking. In fact, it was such a pleasant afternoon that I was astonished when I noticed the golden light of the late afternoon beginning to seep in through the front windows.

As we worked, during those few moments of silence, I found myself fine-tuning my master plan for getting myself inserted back into Sam's life again. I figured I had a few good things in my favor since he'd been in love with me once before. I just needed to focus on those points that had lured him before to hook his interest again.

Cue My Master Plan.

Now I'm fully aware that some narrow-minded people might think my Master Plan would have me graduating from stalking Sam to full-on entrapment. To those people, I would like to point out that once Sam and I were safely married and expecting our firstborn child, *how* we got to that place would be of no real consequence. Just kidding about the firstborn thing. To be frank, every time I imagine where I'm hoping this thing with Sam might lead, it doesn't always include the image of us strolling off into the sunset with matching wedding bands. I'm not sure why that is, because honestly, where else does a happily-ever-after lead?

The basics of my plan hinged on the fact that I knew Sam frequented The Rusty Spoon, the diner located near the police station. He was there for coffee in the morning and then for lunch nearly every day. Half the time he ran by for dinner too. He was practically there more than he was at the police station. And while he was at the diner, there would be no gatekeepers to bar my talking to him.

All I had to do was get a job there as a waitress and begin to wear him down. I considered bouncing my plan off Jim, but he'd been a little prickly lately with regards to Sam. I already knew not to mention my plan to Mary because not only would she be horrified that I still hadn't given up on Sam, but she would be truly mortified at the thought of me waitressing since there seemed to be some stigma attached to the occupation in 1924. No matter. Even without putting it into committee for approval, I was sure my plan was foolproof.

After a few days of my infectious laugh, my batting lashes and general irresistible adorableness, I had no doubt that Sam would remember why he'd fallen in love with me in the first place. A minor fly in this ointment was the fact that I'd never worked as a waitress before but, honestly, how hard could it be?

12

The Rusty Spoon was actually an old-style railroad car built on a truck chassis, with aluminum exterior trim and gleaming chrome accents along the rounded edges. Large windows ran along the front so passersby could look in and see the bustling activity inside. Colorful, almost cartoony signage adorned the walls advertising sandwiches and pies. Diners sat in booths with red leatherette seats. Everything from the tiled floors to the long continuous counter displaying pies under glass domes shined from frequent polishing.

I'd gotten to the diner early to beat the crowd, but let's face it, it was a diner. By seven in the morning, it was crammed full of people eating breakfast. I could only imagine how early the staff must have had to get there. Once inside, I pushed my way past the counter through the swinging doors where I spotted a man in the kitchen who wasn't cooking nor was he wearing an apron. I figured he must be the boss. Unfortunately, I didn't get two words out in my briefly rehearsed elevator speech about why I'd be a great waitress for him before he turned, jerked a none-too-clean apron off a peg and tossed it to me, telling me that if I made it to the end of the day he'd let me do it again tomorrow for money.

Honestly, I wasn't that surprised that the interview process was so slapdash, since in my observation of the existing waitresses at the diner, breathing in and out appeared to be the only real qualification for employment. Both waitresses—Jennie and Eloise as I was soon to learn—eyed me with unconcealed hostility. I guess they were seeing all their tips about to be funneled my way since I was making the effort of wearing makeup and smiling at the diners.

In any case, the two waitresses refused to actually allow me to greet any diners but instead positioned me behind the counter where my only real job was taking down the orders of the barstool patron, then turning around and handing the orders to the short order cook, and finally turning back again to place the plates in front of the diners. An idiot could do it. They didn't even let me handle the cash register. At the end of the day, I hadn't seen Sam and I ended up walking home more exhausted than I can ever remember being.

The next day, I showed up for my first real day of paid waitressing. I'd given myself a pep talk the entire walk from my townhouse to the diner to encourage myself to stand up and demand to be allowed to actually wait on tables. When I got there, my heart was racing with nerves as I looked around the bustling restaurant when I got there to see if I could spot Sam. There was a wide assortment of clientele, from businessmen in woolen three-piece suits and mill factory workers in dusty coveralls chatting loudly over coffee and eggs—the factory machinery must make them hard of hearing—to what looked like Savannah's version of Ladies Who Lunch gossiping over coffee and pie.

I tied a none-too-white apron around my waist, ready for my first day as an official waitress. I picked up my order pad and confidently approached my first table of diners. The sun filtered through the large windows of the diner, casting warm rays onto the checkered tablecloths, and generally painting a very cozy atmosphere. I took a deep breath and with a smile on my face greeted the man and woman sitting in the booth.

"Hi there," I said. "Welcome to The Rusty Spoon. My name is Georgia and I'll be your server today."

The two of them looked at me as if I'd begun spouting Latin. The husband blushed deeply, as if I'd propositioned him, and I could see in the process I'd already pissed off the wife. It occurred to me that none of the other waitresses were identifying themselves, so I guess they didn't do that back in 1924. The couple ordered their food from the menu with stone faces. I scribbled down their orders on my pad, and rushed to the kitchen window to put the order in. The cook—a portly slob of a man named Albie—glowered at me, which prompted me to ask him what part of being asked to cook was a surprise to him since he was in fact the diner's cook. In retrospect, I'd have to say that was a bad first move. I didn't actually see him spit in the food that he plated up for me a few minutes later, but from the howls of outrage and sounds of gagging that came from my table after I delivered the food it was pretty clear that Albie had gotten his own back at me.

(Note to self: There are a few people in life you don't want to cross, and a short-order cook is one of them.)

Luckily for me, the owner of the diner, Charlie Johnson, had stepped out of the diner, so my table's outrage fell on mostly deaf—or in the case of the other waitresses, uncaring—ears. The couple stormed out of the diner without paying—which I was told would come out of my so far nonexistent paycheck—but regardless, somehow, at the end of the day, I still had a job.

13

The next morning, I walked to work with much less enthusiasm. I'd worked two full backbreaking days of serving people and smiling when I wanted to upend platters of meatloaf into people's laps and still there was no sign of Sam. It was so frustrating! This morning, after a particularly exhausting breakfast service, I took my break and realized I was almost shaking with the exertions of my morning's labors. I found a small spot in the kitchen to sit for the brief five minutes I had to relax. I knew I needed to patch up my relationship with Albie and so I spent most of my five minutes attempting to catch his eye and smile apologetically at him. My efforts resulted in a sneer and a big gooey loogie on the floor. So, slow progress on that front. As I sat on my little stool, counting all the areas of my body that ached—and it wasn't even lunch time yet—I suddenly realized that one of the people in the kitchen was someone I knew.

She stood with her back to me at the large industrial sink. She wore a too large blue dress over her thin frame and she was attacking the morning's piles of dirty plates and pots with vigor. Her hair was greying slightly and pulled back into a bun. From where I sat, I could see that years of hard labor had given her muscled arms. Her posture was sloping as she tackled her job with a determination borne from having no other alternative.

It was the attendant from the speakeasy ladies room. I was astonished to see her here. At least her job at the speakeasy was not arduous. Gone was the neat dress and pinafore, the carefully combed hair and impassive expression. Even from where I sat, I could see her arms trembling as she lifted the large pots. A line of perspiration dribbled down the side of her face. I hated to interrupt her to ask her story because I could see she was already looking nervously over her shoulder. The diner's owner—a greasy spindly sort of man with a receding hairline and a permanent scowl on his face—was prowling the kitchen looking for people to scream at. I figured that with the speakeasy being raided she might have lost her job, but I knew for a fact that the club was back in business. So, what was she doing here? Was she working two jobs?

One of the waitresses, Jennie, came back for her break—which was my cue to hop up and get back to work. I gave up my seat and pointed to the woman at the sink.

"How long has she worked here?" I asked in a low voice.

Jennie turned to where I was pointing.

"Ruby? Years, I think," she said.

"I thought I saw her at The Cottonmouth Club in the ladies room," I said.

Jennie gave me a disbelieving look as if to say *You? In the Cottonmouth Club?* But she answered as if she believed me.

"That big Hollywood star what died had her fired," Jennie said with a shrug as if to say these things are to be expected.

I was immediately horrified that Celeste Latour had gotten Ruby fired. What a cow! But I felt a shiver of guilt too. If I hadn't shamed the star like I did, perhaps she wouldn't have lashed out at the poor woman trying to survive on tips in the ladies room.

"Are you going back to work or what?" Jennie asked as she lit a cigarette.

I hurried back to the dining area, where thoughts of poor Ruby were quickly pushed aside by people yelling at me for refills and menus and complaints of how the food was cooked—like I had something to do with that. Within ten minutes, I was perspiring and feeling shaky again. Even though I wasn't doing this for the money, I was still astounded by the fact that I'd worked four straight hours—and this is with most of the tables not having their food defiled by the cook—and yet I still hadn't gotten more than two dimes worth of tips. Now, I know money doesn't have the same value in 1924 as it does in 2024 but still, you'd have to be seriously pathetic not to take a dime left as a tip as a serious insult.

I worked the rest of the afternoon, keeping my eye on the front door for Sam, until I realized that my back was killing me, followed closely by my feet. Ever since the misunderstanding with Albie yesterday, I'd made a point to drip with sweetness when handing my orders to him. While he still glowered at me, I could tell he'd softened toward me somewhat. In any case, there were no more complaints from the tables I waited on. Still, I was beginning to lose some confidence in my Master Plan. Now that I was actually working here it was pretty clear that when Sam finally *did* come in, I wouldn't have time to flirt with him since, now that I remember, he almost always came in during lunchtime when we were slammed.

And then there was the very unappealing thought of my coming back here tomorrow and doing this gig over and over again. I physically hurt everywhere. I was getting paid next to nothing. And I really didn't have the patience for people who couldn't make up their minds before then spilling coffee all over themselves and their table with exhausting regularity. As I tried to massage a very tight muscle in my back with my hand, I resigned myself to needing to come up with some other way to get Sam's attention. Maybe I could get arrested again? Just as I was smiling at this ridiculous but tempting thought, two uniformed police officers walked through the door.

I frowned when I saw them because it has been my experience that the uniformed police on the force tend to eat their lunch from brown bags that they brought from home. Unless it was a special occasion eating in a diner was definitely out of their financial purview. Because of that, it's possible that when I saw them, I knew on some level that they weren't here for eating.

I watched them scan the room and when they saw me, they seemed to lock in. Without even knowing I was doing it, I took several steps back. When they began to advance on me I turned to walk away, hoping to blend into the bustling lunchtime crowd. But just then the diners at one nearby table noticed me and called out for more coffee, causing me to hesitate. As I turned back towards the officers, their faces were impassive but determined. One of them spoke, his voice low but authoritative.

"Georgia Belle?" he said sternly. "You are under arrest for the murder of Celeste Latour."

14

Sam had been in Chief Willis' office many times. Most of those times had not been pleasant. Not that his boss had ever called him in to reprimand him, but Willis wasn't the kind of man to hand out compliments or atta-boys. Sam usually had a sickening feeling deep in the pit of his stomach when he was in this room as he did now. The Chief sat behind his large oak desk, his hands folded as he nodded his head as if approving Sam's choice of clothing.

"Good work, Bohannon," he said. "It's a pity you couldn't get there before the press reported it was natural causes but never mind. You got there in the end."

Sam stared at the man, his stomach continuing to churn. He knew this meeting would be half insult and half praise. He wasn't sure how this had all come to a head. One minute Sam was entertaining a mere feeling about Celeste Latour's death. And the next, he was suggesting an autopsy—in spite of pushback from the victim's family—should be performed. If he had done nothing, the star's death would not have been labeled suspicious, and he wouldn't be here on the rough end of Willis telling him how disappointed he was in him.

Why had Sam decided to push for the autopsy when her husband had deemed it unnecessary? Maybe it was her youth, her very vibrancy on the silver screen—all things that were subjective and indefinable—but he'd just had a feeling that Celeste Latour's death was something other than how it looked. Call it a policeman's instinct. Sam had felt an urge to tell Georgia about how it had all come about. She had trouble respecting his natural gifts as a detective. But this was something she would have to admit showed his skill. Unfortunately, he wasn't in a position to ask for her praise or respect.

While he should be celebrating the fact that the autopsy came back and confirmed what Sam had started to suspect —that Celeste Latour had been murdered, he was in no position to rejoice. He was aware that if it wasn't for the fact that he already had someone under arrest for the crime, this meeting with Willis would be going a very different way. For now, he forced himself to push thoughts of Georgia away. Either she had a good explanation for the evidence against her or she didn't. He'd cross that bridge when he came to it and pray it wasn't what it looked like.

One step at a time, Bohannon. If she's innocent, it will come out. The truth always comes out.

He found himself wiping a line of perspiration from his brow as he thought of his last murder case.

Except when it doesn't.

As he stood before his boss, he felt the conflict continue to battle inside him. On the one side he felt a natural pride that he'd thought to push for the autopsy.

That took skill and a superior perception that nobody else had shown but himself.

Yet on the other side was the fact that his gut was swirling with nausea at what that intuition had cost him.

Georgia.

"It was a group effort, sir," Sam said, staring fixedly at a spot above the Chief's head.

That was true. No sooner had Sam been handled proof that the death was suspicious than he'd realized how cold he'd be going into the case. Three days late! When his sergeant had handed him the photograph that allowed him to stand here right now proudly, fully deserving of his superior's accolades.

Except he was sweating like he was in a sauna.

"Modesty won't get you promoted, son. Take the praise," Willis said.

"Yessir."

"Unfortunately, the press are going to eat this up," Willis said. "Are you ready for that?"

Sam forced his face not to reveal the disgust he felt under the Chief's beady stare. Willis would concentrate on the publicity angle of course, not the matter of justice.

"We are, sir," Sam said.

"Good, good. There might be a little something extra for you in your pay packet this month, Bohannon. Don't argue. You earned it. Now let's lock down that confession, eh? Wrap this up while the body's still warm."

The man laughed at his own joke and Sam fought to keep his lunch down.

∾

The bare-bones interview room did little to calm my nerves. Naturally the whole point of the room wasn't to calm anyone's nerves. Especially not guilty people or even innocent people who've been dragged into this room in handcuffs and made to wait. Two metal chairs sat before a scarred wooden table under a single glaring electric bulb. The stained concrete walls offered no distraction as the moments ticked by like hours.

I felt my fingers grip the edge of the table, as my mind raced through all the possibilities of why I had been arrested. Each footstep in the hallway outside the room made me jump. I did my best to steady myself with logic. I knew I had done nothing wrong. But logic held little power over emotions siting in this cold, impersonal room. Dread coiled in my stomach as I waited.

By the time the doorknob rattled, I felt myself quaking in my skin. Sam walked into the room. My first thought when I saw him was that he was so handsome, so tall, so sure of himself. A big part of me wanted to jump up and throw my arms around him. In spite of myself I had every expectation that he was here to help me.

He disabused me of that notion in the next ten seconds.

He dropped a folder on the table and sat down in the chair opposite me.

"What the hell, Georgia?" he asked, his eyes probing me sadly.

"That's just what I was going to ask you, Sam," I said, steeling my spine.

If I was going to have to do this on my own, then I needed to toughen up. In that moment, I felt a murky mixture of emotions. I loved this man. I love him still. And yet I was all too aware of the mistakes he'd made in the cases he'd handled before now. I had been there with him, covering for him. I knew him. He didn't see things. Or he only saw what the average person saw. A good detective needed to see the subtext, see the entire game board at a glance. Sam was a terrible chess player. He only saw one move at a time. When he latched onto a suspect, he tried to explain away any inconsistencies in evidence in order to hang onto the suspect no matter what. He wasn't logical. That's what I needed to remember. Sam's slipshod tendencies would be my salvation.

And then I would lose him forever.

"Can I ask you what you were doing at the Cottonmouth Club?" he asked, folding his hands over the file in front of him, his voice almost conversational and not at all as if he was about to launch into a brutal interrogation of a murder suspect.

I looked at him in bewilderment.

"You already know about that," I said. "I was arrested in the raid that—"

"I'm not talking about that night."

He flipped open the folder.

"I'm talking about Saturday the fifth of April."

I felt an uncomfortable fluttering in my chest.

"I...I wasn't there then," I said. "I never went back to the club after the raid."

"We have witnesses who say otherwise."

"Then they are misremembering," I said.

"Six witnesses are misremembering?" he asked, leaning in close.

Six people saw me the night Celeste Latour was killed?

The fluttering in my chest turned into a painful tightening sensation.

"So if you weren't there, where were you that night?" Sam asked.

I looked at him in building distress and my mind began to race in circles. I'm sure to him it looked as if I was desperately trying to come up with a plausible story, and then it hit me. Celeste Latour was killed the night I transported back from 2024.

My mouth was dry, and I could feel a killer headache coming on. I didn't have an alibi. I quickly ran through the likelihood of getting a hold of Jim or Mary and getting them to lie and say they were with me that night but, knowing Sam, I wouldn't get any phone call and therefore no chance to establish a fake alibi.

"I don't remember," I mumbled, looking away.

He nodded as if he had expected nothing else.

"So, to be clear," he said, "you have no alibi for the time in question."

He was so cold, so robotic, that I couldn't believe that this was the same man who had asked me to be his wife only six months ago.

"Gosh, Sam, are you enjoying this?" I asked, my eyes stinging with tears.

My accusation shook him. He ran a hand over his face as if to gather himself together.

"No, I'm not enjoying this, Miss Belle," he said. "But I can't ignore the evidence. You need to tell me a different scenario than what I am seeing."

"I don't have an alibi. But you have no evidence that I killed Celeste Latour. What was my motive?"

"I'm sure that will be revealed in time," he said.

"Who are these six witnesses? I don't know six people in all of Savannah. How do they know me?"

"They identified you," he said.

"Identified me? How? Was I a part of a covert line-up I had no idea about?"

"No," he said, sliding a photograph across the table to me. "They identified you from this photograph taken the night of the murder."

It took me a moment to realize what I was seeing and when I did, I nearly groaned out loud. I felt like telling Sam to go ahead and lock me up and throw away the key because there was no way I was going to be able to explain what I was looking at. The photograph clearly showed me—and there was no mistake it was me—on my knees wearing latex yoga pants and a midriff top on the floor of the Cottonmouth Club. The photographer's strobe must have been the bright flash I remembered seeing just before I finished transporting back from 2024 to my townhouse on East Peter's Street.

I slumped in my chair.

"Miss Belle?" Sam said. "Georgia?"

"I can't explain this," I said.

He sighed and took the photo back.

"So you admit it is you in the photograph?"

I looked at him, suddenly angry that it was him who was doing this to me. Because I couldn't tell him that I came from the future, I was going to be defenseless against a charge for a murder I didn't commit.

"What do you want me to say, Sam?" I said. "No comment."

His eyes widened because of course *no comment* was an admission of guilt and they knew that even back in 1924. Sam tucked the photograph back in the folder and rested his hands on it again. It didn't matter what happened now. I was done. Fully and completely.

But Sam wasn't done.

"There was also a note, in the victim's handwriting," he said in a soft voice, "saying she was afraid for her life because of you."

"Because of me," I said dully. "Someone she met one night in the ladies room."

"Two women have given statements that they heard you threaten the victim that night in the ladies' room," he said.

I took in a long inhale and let it out slowly.

"No comment," I said listlessly.

15

That night, I sat huddled in the corner of a dingy cell, pulling a threadbare shawl that I'd found on the bench in the cell around myself. The night stretched endlessly before me, each tick of the clock felt like an hour. This time, I wasn't sharing my cell with people dressed in heels and fox fur coats. Shadowy figures moved around the other cells, an occasional cough or groan echoed down the corridor. The stench of unwashed bodies, urine and stale tobacco clung heavily in the damp air. My stomach churned both from hunger and nerves.

Sleep was impossible on the hard wooden plank that served as my bed. I shifted, my bones aching from the unforgiving surface. Each creak of the building had me sitting bolt upright, scanning for any sign of danger in the inky darkness. Dread consumed me as I pondered my fate come morning. But for now, all I could do was hug myself and stare out through the small, barred window at a sky just beginning to lighten. It was hard to believe this was happening to me, but the evidence that Sam had was hard to refute.

On the one hand, the witnesses and the photograph might prove I was at the Cottonmouth Club that night but that was all it proved. On its own, the photograph wasn't particularly damning. The note, however, written in Celeste's handwriting and referencing me as someone she feared for her life from was another thing altogether. Since I knew Celeste Latour didn't know me from Adam's house cat —our little dust up in the ladies' room last week notwithstanding—it meant the note had to be manufactured by the actual killer.

Try explaining that to Sam, though.

I could still see the sharp disappointment in his face as he sat across from me in the interview room. If I hadn't been so sick with fear about what was going to happen to me, I'd have spared some emotion to be a little disappointed in *him* too. Honestly, *this* was all the credit he was going to give me?

I've literally solved *two* major cases for him that, if not for me, would've sent two innocent men to their deaths. Forget the fact that Sam got major accolades and commendations that he hadn't deserved. I wonder if he ever thinks about that? I wonder if he might actually resent me for the work I did to make all that happen. I felt a wave of futility sift through me. In any case, I deserved more than he was giving me right now.

Why was he so eager to believe I was guilty? The evidence wasn't all that compelling. Was he just determined to shine the brass of the rank above him that he wasn't that concerned with getting it wrong?

Again?

Suddenly, I heard footsteps coming down the stone walkway to my cell and a jangling of keys. A figure approached carrying a lantern. I stood up slowly on unsteady legs, my heart leaping in hope and fear.

"Georgia Belle?" a gruff voice called out. I managed a weak "Yes" in response. Heavy keys slid into the lock on my cell with a clank and the cell door creaked open. Shielding my eyes from the sudden light, I peered out. A stocky policeman loomed in the doorway, his cap pulled down low over stern features. But his eyes held no malice as he addressed me.

"You've been bailed out," he said. "Come on, let's go."

Weak with relief, I gathered the shawl tightly around me and followed him to the same processing counter where I'd been brought in nearly twenty-four hours earlier. Once again, I saw Jim O'Connell waiting for me.

I had no expectation that I was going to be allowed bail on a murder charge. Right then I knew it was Sam who agreed to it. I wanted to hate him, but this meant that he was trying to help me. Or at least trying to be fair.

I walked over to Jim, and instantly felt anger vibrate off him. Whether that anger was directed at me or the police, I couldn't tell. Neither of us spoke while he finished my release paperwork and then, with a hand on my elbow, he led me outside.

Fresh air hit my face like a cleansing breeze as we emerged into the morning. I turned to him.

"It's a murder charge," I said. "How did you possibly —"

"Wait until we're out of ear shot," he said brusquely.

Jim's brand-new 1923 Model T was parked in front of the station. He opened the door and I saw Mary sitting inside. Of course. Only Mary had the money to post bail on a murder charge. It must have cost her thousands.

"Mary," I said weakly as I climbed into the car and was instantly folded into her arms.

She didn't speak, and I felt her tremors as she held me.

Behind me, Jim climbed into the driver's seat. I pulled free of Mary's arms.

"You know I didn't do this," I said to her.

"Don't be ridiculous," she said, pulling out a handkerchief to dab at her eyes. "Of course you didn't. I could murder that Sam Bohannon."

"What evidence do they have?" Jim asked as he pulled away from the curb. His eyes caught mine in the rearview mirror.

"None really," I said. "It's all circumstantial."

"The things you say," he said, shaking his head, amazed I suppose that I even knew the term.

"They have witnesses saying they saw me there the night of the murder," I said.

"But that's not true, right?" Jim asked. "So why would the witnesses lie?"

"They're not lying," I said and rubbed my temples. "I'll explain it all, but I could use a single hour of sleep in my own bed first."

I shot a quick glance at Mary who instantly interpreted it as my not being able to explain the evidence because I'd been in the middle of a time-traveling moment. There was no way I could tell Jim—or anybody else in this timeline—what really happened.

"The papers said she died of natural causes," Mary said.

"That's what everyone thought," I said. "But the autopsy showed she'd been poisoned."

Mary sucked in a shocked gasp of breath.

"You'll need a good lawyer," she said.

I nodded. But a lawyer wouldn't be able to undo the proof of my having been there when Celeste Latour was killed or the fact of her damning note. What I really needed was to find out who had really killed her. I looked at Jim who was stealing glances at me through the rearview mirror. He looked very concerned, as he often does when we're together. Honestly, half the time I think he's figured out my secret—or at least he was trying to—but so far there weren't too many people who would attribute unexplained, eccentric behavior to time travel.

Or at least it wouldn't be their first assumption.

16

I spent the rest of the day in bed. Jim had suggested that he stick around but I told him it wasn't necessary. Even so, Mary stayed while I slept and basically spent the day dusting and watering plants in the living room. It was fall and since I'd yet to hire a cook—believing honestly that I didn't need one just for me—she'd brought over supper and set it out on a small table in front of the fireplace.

The fact that I was living here alone without servants had become a bone of contention between me and Mary. First, she doesn't understand how I can manage alone even if I don't need people to dress me. And secondly, and probably more importantly, unless you're an elderly spinster, it's just not the *done* thing, an unmarried woman living alone. Mary gets away with it because her family has been in the community for generations and because she has a live-in butler and cook.

By the time I made my way downstairs after a deliciously hot bath, wrapped in a fluffy robe that I'd brought with me from Kohls in 2024, Mary was decanting the wine in front of the fireplace. She gave me a disapproving look since wearing nightclothes outside the bedroom was something she and everyone else in this time disapproved of, but the look was quickly erased when she saw my face.

"You look better," she said, nodding.

"I feel better," I said. "I do not recommend spending a night in jail."

"I'll keep that in mind."

I looked at the table groaning with food: buttermilk biscuits, fresh churned butter with honey, slabs of meatloaf, stewed okra, and fried green tomatoes. I'd already seen the peach pie cooling on the counter in the kitchen as I came down the stairs.

"Omigosh, Mary, did you do all this? I didn't even think I had enough pots or pans to manage this!"

"You probably don't," she said. "I had Cook make it and Seamus walked it down."

"Well, it all looks amazing," I said as I sat down and put my cloth napkin on my lap.

The small fire in the grate felt so luxurious, taking the chill off the house and providing a flicker of visual comfort.

"I feel so taken care of," I said. "Everything is just perfect."

She poured our wine before filling her plate.

"How are you going to explain how you were at the club during the murder?" she asked.

I can't tell you what a relief it is that someone finally knows my secret. Up until last year, I'd have had to prevaricate with Mary about how it was I came to be in the club at that moment. Now she was able to be a true friend who knew all my mysteries.

I took a long restorative sip of the wine. Seamus must have brought it too since I knew I didn't have any this good.

"I don't know," I said. "I think I'm just going to have to find the real killer."

"I thought you might say that," she said. "You should hire Jim to help you."

"I'll think about it," I said as I helped myself to a healthy portion of the fried green tomatoes with its accompanying remoulade sauce.

"I know you worry about his feelings for you," she said.

"Yes, and also the fact that I can't be honest with him about certain stuff." I raised a knowing eyebrow at her.

"That's irrelevant," she said with a sniff. "He can still knock on doors with you and protect you if need be. He can do the legwork for investigating this case. He doesn't need to know about the time travel business in order to get the other stuff right."

I smiled as I listened. Just as certain phrases from this timeline like *rigamarole* and the *bee's knees* had been seeping into my vocabulary over the last eighteen months, so Mary was beginning to pick up words from me that nobody else used, words like *stuff* and *cool*. It pleased me so much because I felt as if we were truly meeting each other in the middle across the divide. A little of her world was rubbing off on me and vice versa.

"I have to say," she said, "I was shocked that Sam was so willing to believe your involvement in this. Is there more evidence against you that you haven't spoken of?"

I grimaced. Sam's eagerness to arrest me—in spite of my being someone he'd once been engaged to—had bothered me too.

"There's a photograph showing me at the club during the time of the murder."

Mary made a face. "How did that happen?"

"I'm not really sure. It's like I made an unintended side trip when I came back from 2024 this time."

"And you went to the Cottonmouth Club?"

"It was just a handful of seconds, but evidently it was right around the time of the murder."

"And you were photographed during this time," Mary said, frowning.

"Not only that, but Sam said they found a note written in Celeste's handwriting saying she was afraid for her life because of me."

Mary raised an eyebrow.

"Didn't you say you argued with her that night?" she asked.

Now it was my turn to frown. *What is she suggesting?*

"Not the night she was killed," I said. "We argued the week before."

"Well, clearly whoever faked the note was someone who overheard that argument or knew about it."

I smiled then. I love Mary. I should have known she believed in me regardless of the evidence. Not only that, but she made a great point. Whoever had tried to frame me must be someone close to Mary to have seen or known of my brief altercation with her. That meant one of her entourage—either her husband, personal assistant or agent.

"That's brilliant," I said to her, grinning once I realized she'd essentially just laid out my three main suspects.

Mary smiled back, pink in the cheeks and I could tell my praise meant a lot to her.

"I agree with you about Sam, though," I said. "And I have no real explanation for that. All I can think is that he's under a lot of pressure to solve this case quickly. Celeste Latour was a very big Hollywood movie star."

"I wouldn't be so quick to let him off the hook," Mary said.

"He does have a good collection of very believable evidence against me," I said. "I can't blame him for that."

"Except you're innocent," she countered. "All the evidence in the world against an innocent person has to be a misdirection."

"Yeah, but *you* know the evidence is irrelevant because you know the truth about me."

"Jim doesn't know," she pointed out. "And *he* still thinks you're innocent."

"Maybe," I said. "But it's possible Jim doesn't care if I'm innocent."

"You could do worse than be with someone who thinks you're amazing no matter what. Remind me again of that phrase from your time?"

"Unconditional love," I said.

"Mm-mmm, I really like that."

"You can't use it here," I reminded her. "You'll sound odd."

"You mean like you do?" she said with a smile.

"That's different," I said. "I don't care if people think I'm weird. You have to live here."

That wasn't the right thing to say because Mary and I have had many anguished conversations about whether or not I intended to stay in 1924 or go back to my own time. Honestly, I was breaking my brain trying to make up my mind. There were so many amazing benefits to each time for different reasons. Although I have to say that my friendship with Mary counts for staying much more than any of my other reasons for leaving.

"But back to Jim," I said, eager to change the subject. "I will use him, but sparingly."

"Have you ever thought about telling him about…your secret?" she asked as she topped up both our wine glasses.

"Not seriously, no," I said. "You are my dearest friend, Mary, and even you had trouble with it."

She shrugged.

"Ah, yes, but now it is…how do you put it? No big deal."

I laughed then and she joined in. Regardless of the fact that I was being charged with first-degree murder and was living in a time a hundred years before my own, I found that at that moment I couldn't remember feeling happier or closer to anyone in my life.

17

The next morning, I eased into my day by doing a few things around the house and cleaning up some of the clutter and trash produced by the work that Jim and I had done in the living room a few days earlier. By the time evening came, my house was basically in order, and I was feeling stronger and more clear-headed about the direction I needed to take to prove my innocence. Jim and I had made arrangements by phone to go to the Cottonmouth Club tonight to see if we could interview any witnesses. I wanted to impress upon him that this was not a date but, in the end, I decided it didn't matter. I knew he was just as committed as I was to finding evidence to clear my name and for now our mutual goal was enough.

The sun had already set by the time Jim and I made our way down the dimly lit alley behind Bay Street where the Cottonmouth Club was located. Sounds of laughter and jazz music floated out ahead of us, guiding our path. It was amazing to me that everything seemed to be business as usual—not only after a recent police raid, but after a murder too. Clearly, if the club *had* closed down, it hadn't been for long.

We came to the same inconspicuous side door that I'd gone through before when I first laid eyes on Celeste Latour and her group. Jim knocked in a particular rhythm and the door creaked open a crack as a gruff voice started to demand our business. When the doorman saw Jim's face, the door opened wider to a revelry of smoke and sound. How was it the doorman knew Jim? That surprised me and I made a mental point to ask him about it later.

Inside, couples two-stepped to piano tunes in the center of the club while others huddled over small tables with servers weaving expertly through the crowd balancing contraband drinks aloft. I looked around for anyone who looked familiar while Jim led us to a shadowed booth toward the back. As we made our way to our seats, I grabbed his arm and nodded across the room. Celeste's hulking bodyguard was at the bar, nursing a drink.

Though easily past forty, the arms of the man revealed muscles from under his rolled-up shirt sleeves. He sported a bulbous nose that had been broken more than once and thin lips that I was willing to bet rarely smiled.

"That's the bodyguard," I said to Jim.

He turned in the direction I indicated and then swore. I glanced at him.

"You know him?" I asked.

"Patrick Murphy. He's a cop. He must have been moonlighting as a bodyguard."

I frowned. Surely Sam knew about this man's extracurricular activities. Presumably he'd been questioned in regard to the murder. A deeply unsettling feeling developed in my gut as we moved toward Murphy. He looked up as we approached. Small eyes glinted with cunning under heavy brows, seeming to take stock of everyone around him out of what was probably an occupational habit. Out of his police uniform now, his bulky presence filled the room, imposing and inescapable, like an entire squad rolled into one massive man.

Even so, I saw a flicker of worry cross his face before the neutral mask took hold again.

"What do you want?" he snarled at us. "Hey, don't I know you?" He peered at Jim.

"I'm a friend of your boss, Sam Bohannon," Jim said. "Why don't you tell us what you were doing the night Celeste Latour was murdered?"

Murphy scowled.

"Wasn't my fault," he said, baring his teeth in barely suppressed anger.

I leaned in closer to make myself heard over the noise.

"Weren't you supposed to protect her?" I asked.

He stuck his chin out defiantly, his face reddening.

"Even I gotta take a leak once in a while."

If he hoped to shock me by his coarse language, he was sorely disappointed.

"So, you were in the gents when she was killed?" Jim asked. "Pretty coincidental."

"I don't know who youse are," Murphy said angrily. "But the detectives on the case cleared me of having anything to do with it."

"By *detectives*, do you mean your pals on the force?" I asked pointedly.

"Just coz I got friends don't mean I'm not innocent," he said sullenly.

"Celeste Latour trusted you with her life," Jim said. "And she probably paid you top dollar. Now she's dead."

I have to admit, this line of attack was better than

anything I would've come up with. Jim was shaming the man for not doing his job—the least of his sins, unless he was the killer. And it seemed to be working.

"Look, I don't know any more than you do," Murphy said morosely, turning back to his drink. "I told her husband to keep an eye on her while I went to the gents. When I came back, she was on the floor."

I shuddered at his words.

Could it really have happened that quickly?

"How long were you gone?" Jim asked.

"Two minutes, tops."

"Did you notice anyone looking at her?"

"Hey, she was a big movie star. Of course people were gonna look at her."

"You know what I mean."

"No, man. That's my job, isn't it? Watching for people looking at her the wrong way. I'm telling you there was nothing like that."

My shoulders sagged a bit in disappointment. I told myself that not hitting gold with the very first witness we interviewed didn't mean we weren't on the right track. But still, we'd gotten very little new information out of her bodyguard. It made me wonder what this guy had told Sam. Surely, he'd been interrogated within an inch of his life? Or had he?

I'm convinced the Old Boy's network got its start in the twenties. Law and order only went as far as who knew whom. Especially in a town like Savannah. And while this guy didn't look to be ranked high enough to warrant special favors, I more than anyone knew the almost criminal bias cops took when it came to protecting their own.

18

I didn't feel like giving up and heading home just yet, so I talked Jim into hanging around for a drink. I could tell he was uneasy—even though clearly, he was something just short of a regular here. I assumed his uneasiness had to do with worry about the place getting raided with me—a murder suspect out on bail—getting caught up in the dragnet once more.

After talking to Murphy, we split up and did a pretty thorough scan of the place but didn't find anyone else who might have seen something that night. Even the bartenders and waiters claimed to have seen nothing. When we slipped into a booth—with Jim still looking all around as if he expected a raid at any moment—a waitress came over to take our orders. She was one I hadn't talked to and I recognized her from my first night at the club.

She was in her mid-forties and looked tired and I wondered what unfortunate stroke of fate had driven her to work in an illegal drinking den. After we ordered our drinks, I held up a five-dollar bill.

"Listen," I said, "I was here a week ago and there was a black woman in the ladies room, but I didn't see her today."

That was a lie of course since I hadn't visited the ladies room this trip.

"You mean Ruby," the waitress said with no expression on her face. She glanced over at the bar where I saw the bartender frowning at her.

Clearly, she was meant to keep moving and taking orders. I pulled out a ten-dollar bill—which is worth like a hundred dollars in these times. I put it and the five on her tray.

"Tell me why she's not here anymore," I said.

The waitress didn't even bother glancing at the bartender this time but slid the bills off the tray and into her apron pocket.

"Ruby got canned when that movie star told the boss to get rid of her."

I frowned. I hated that that appeared to be true. Mostly because I was at least partially to blame.

"What can you tell me about her?" I asked.

"About Ruby?" The waitress shrugged and shifted her tray in her hand as she thought. "She's got a husband who lost his arm in some kind of mill accident a few years ago. He can't work so it's up to Ruby."

"I saw her at The Rusty Spoon," I prompted.

"Yeah, but it ain't enough. She's only washing dishes there. No tips. Which is too bad because she's an amazing cook."

"Where does she live?" I asked, aware now of Jim's curious attention to my questions.

"In the colored ghetto last I heard. But I think they're being evicted. Or maybe that's already happened. I'm sorry but I have to get back to work."

I slipped her another ten dollars and her eyes widened.

"Thank you for your time," I said.

As she walked away to get our drinks, Jim cocked his head to study me silently.

"I got into an argument with Celeste Latour in the ladies room," I said, "because she was being incredibly rude to the restroom attendant."

"And so, she got Ruby fired," he said. "That's not your fault. No more than it's your fault her husband got hurt and can't work."

"Unless he's brain damaged," I said. Having only one arm shouldn't keep him from working."

Jim shrugged.

"Why would anyone hire a one-armed man when they can get a fellow with two arms just as easily? You can't save the world, Georgia."

"But you can try," I said firmly.

The air around us was thick with cigarette and cigar smoke, mingling with the smells of spilled liquor and perfume. Low lighting from wall sconces and table lamps seemed to create an intimate atmosphere. I found myself relaxing for the first time all night. When the waitress came back to our booth with our drinks, I could tell she was hoping for another tip. I didn't disappoint her. I pulled out another ten dollars and laid it on her tray.

"The movie star who was killed here," I started.

"I didn't work that night," she said quickly, her eyes on the money but not touching it.

"That's okay," I said. "But you saw her with her entourage, right? On the other nights she was here?"

She seemed to unkink with relief that she'd be able to earn the ten dollars after all.

"That's right," she said, taking the bill.

"Did you hear anything? I mean among her group? I've worked as a waitress myself. I know sometimes it's hard not to overhear."

That was technically not a lie, since I'd only worked a day and a half as a waitress, but I wanted to make her feel at ease if I was going to ask her to admit to eavesdropping.

"I might have accidentally overheard a few things," she said warily.

"Like what?" I asked.

I fully expected her to tell me things she'd heard Celeste say or possibly her personal assistant Millie or her husband or agent. She surprised me.

"It was that bodyguard of hers," she said, her eyes flickering to the bar where the very same bodyguard sat drinking heavily.

"Really?" I said.

Because a bodyguard's job—beyond protecting his charge—was basically to blend into the background and be unobtrusive, I was shocked that Murphy was the one the waitress had overheard.

"What did he say?" Jim asked.

Now the waitress was really nervous. I could tell by the way she fingered the money that a part of her was tempted to give it back.

But that part was shouted down by the bigger part of her that really wanted it.

"He said he was going to fix her wagon."

19

Now I'm not an etymologist but even I know the phrase *I'm going to fix your wagon* is a threat. I knew it, the waitress knew it, Jim knew it and I'm pretty sure the victim to whom it was said knew it. When the waitress walked away from our booth, I turned to Jim with excitement.

"He threatened her!" I whispered loudly.

His face was tense as he glanced at the bar where Murphy sat. Together, we watched the burly policeman push away from the bar and stumble to the exit.

"I wonder if anyone can vouch for him being in the men's room at the time of the murder," I said.

"Good question."

"Why would he threaten her?"

"Well, you did say she treated people badly. Murphy is not really a servant. He's a decorated police officer. Perhaps she insulted him."

"So, you don't think the *fix your wagon* comment meant murder?"

He shrugged.

"Frankly, it's not much to go on."

"No," I agreed. "Not all by itself it isn't. But now we've got someone with opportunity and with this threat, possibly motive, too."

"Maybe."

It was annoying that Jim wasn't more impressed with what we'd learned. The truth is I really didn't think Patrick Murphy looked like the murdering type. To me he looked like a ham-fisted bruiser who was used to pushing people around in keeping with his role as a cop. The only thing that held me back from believing he might be the killer was the poisoning aspect of the murder. For someone who was used to bulldozing his way through life and other's people's civil rights, dropping a few pills into someone's drink—if that's how it happened—felt way too subtle for him.

Jim finished his drink and got up, reaching for his wallet.

"Let's call it for tonight," he said.

I wasn't sure what was wrong with him, but his attitude had definitely changed in the last hour. I'm not sure if it was because I'd taken the lead in questioning the waitress, but in any event he was right about one thing. It was late and we were both tired.

∼

The next morning, I was up early and headed straight to the police station to see if I could get a meeting with Sam to ask him about Patrick Murphy. I'd thought about going with Jim but after our silent drive home last night, I decided to go alone. You don't need to be a master detective to know that Jim was jealous of Sam or at the very least uncomfortable being around me and Sam together.

The two-story brick police station on Oglethorpe

Street has large windows in the front of the building allowing light into the main waiting room which is crammed with wooden chairs and benches. I've spent a lot of time in this building. Back in 2024 the building itself was demolished decades earlier and was now a Honey Baked Ham store. I always thought that was too bad since, as I looked at it now, its exterior was absolutely stunning with curlicues and figurines carved into the brickwork. It's true what they say that most American cities cared about what their government buildings looked like in the old days. This building should have been on the historic register in Savannah. It certainly would've been if it had survived.

I'd tried calling Sam first to see if I could get an appointment, but no one would connect me, so my only other option was to go to the waiting room until the receptionist took pity on me. I knew someone would mention to Sam that I was waiting. I had to hope he would be curious enough to come see me for himself. I settled into one of the extremely uncomfortable wooden benches with a paperback book I'd brought back with me, *The Girl Who Kicked the Hornet's Nest* and began to wait. For whatever reason, I didn't have to wait long this morning before Sam appeared and beckoned to me from the hallway. I expected to be taken to his office, but he stopped in the hall.

"What is it, Georgia?" he asked coldly, folding his arms across his chest.

I looked around the hall as uniformed policemen walked up and down the corridor. I half expected to see Patrick Murphy himself. There was no reason why I shouldn't have. He was definitely still active on the force.

"How are you doing?" I asked.

I thought Sam looked tired. For someone who must have

made his superiors very happy by getting an early collar for a high-profile murder, he didn't look very happy himself.

"I'm fine. Why are you here?"

Enough small talk, I guess.

"I wanted to thank you for allowing Mary to put up bail for me," I said.

"If you run, you'll only hurt her."

That's cold. Nothing like somebody holding your friends hostage to instill confidence in you. I swallowed down my burgeoning anger.

"I need to ask you about Patrick Murphy," I said.

He made an impatient face and uncrossed his arms so he could place his hands on his hips. A stance, I have to say, which felt very combative.

"What do you expect, Sam?" I said in exasperation. "You arrested me for a murder I didn't commit. Am I supposed to just sit back and wait for you to slap the cuffs on me again?"

"So dramatic," he muttered, but he was looking at the floor as if possibly ashamed of what I was saying.

"I'm trying to find out who killed Celeste Latour," I said. "I need your help."

"We're on opposite sides of the situation," he said, still not looking at me. "I can't help you."

"I'm just asking if you've spoken to Murphy? Does he have an alibi? Because I talked to someone at the club who overheard him threaten the victim."

Sam snapped his head around to look at me. Now I had his attention.

"You should not be at the Cottonmouth Club," he growled. "Aren't you in enough trouble?"

"Sam, I'm trying to clear my name. The witnesses who saw anything worth seeing were at the Cottonmouth Club. What do you suggest I do?"

"I suggest you trust your lawyer. I assume you've hired one?"

"I've hired a private investigator instead."

I hit a nerve there. He knew I was referring to Jim. I'd promised myself I wouldn't use the Intel that Jim had given me about Sam's possible jealousy against him, but Sam made it impossible for me not to. He stiffened visibly. His eyes became instantly shuttered and unreadable. But a telltale muscle twitched in his jaw.

"I'm sorry I can't help you," he said, turning on his heel.

"*Are* you?" I called after his retreating back as he marched off down the hallway.

I waited, hoping he'd turn around, but he didn't. Instead the waiting room receptionist suddenly materialized to direct me out of the hall and out of the station itself.

20

The mahogany table in Mary's dining room gleamed in the light of the beautiful and intricate crystal chandelier that hung overhead. The table was meticulously set with Mary's finest china and lead-crystal stemware even though it was just me, Mary, and Jim for dinner. It wasn't the first time we'd dined together but it was usually in the kitchen. I know Mary likes her pretty things and maybe she just wanted to enjoy them for an evening. I watched Jim to see if he looked uncomfortable, but he acted as if he ate this way all the time.

After my brief and very unsatisfactory conversation with Sam this morning I'd toyed with the idea of going back to the Cottonmouth Club to see if I could talk to anyone else. But Jim was busy today doing his real work and I wasn't eager to go without him.

Mary's two cantankerous servants, Seamus the butler and the woman we all called Cook, although her name was Lenore, came through the swinging door, moving in perfectly synchronized steps bearing platters of steaming food which they laid before us with practiced movements. If

I had to guess, I'd say that Mary had organized this formal dinner as much for Seamus and Cook as for us.

Outside, night had fully fallen. After the two servants disappeared we three passed bowls and platters around the table.

"This all looks delicious," Jim said to Mary.

"I'm glad you think so," she said, pinking with pleasure at his compliment.

"How was your day today?" I asked, spooning a substantial serving of creamed corn onto my plate.

"I'm afraid I'm having very little luck finding you staff," Mary said with a sigh as she handed me the breadbasket.

She had taken it upon herself to interview people to staff my townhouse—a cook and a butler.

"I think it's important that the two work well together," she said. "They don't necessarily have to be husband and wife, but it helps if they know each other."

"Do I really need two people?" I asked with a sigh. "I mean, how hard is it to answer my own door?"

"That's not the point," Mary said with obvious patience. "It's the fact of being *seen* answering your own door."

"But I don't care about stuff like that."

"A butler does other things. He lifts heavy items for the cook, he collects the mail, he runs off hoboes, he walks your dog."

I could only imagine how unfulfilled and desperate someone would have to be to spend their life doing such mundane tasks. As if she could read my mind, Mary spoke again.

"You have to remember where these people come from," she said. "You're not hiring Harvard graduates. You're hiring people grateful for a day's work and a roof over their head."

"Sounds positively Dickensian."

"Be that as it may. What about you two? Any progress on the case?" she said glancing at Jim and smiling as if to include him.

"Not really," I said, rubbing a hand across my eyes. "Every time we think we're getting somewhere, we run into a roadblock."

"How colorfully you speak," Mary said wryly.

"It's early days yet," Jim said. "We're just at the beginning."

"So, who is it you suspect?" Mary asked.

"Well, there's Latour's bodyguard," I said. "He looks shifty, and he was overheard threatening her."

"My," Mary said. "That sounds promising."

"Yeah, but that's about it so far."

"I'm afraid Sam will want to move ahead pretty quickly," Jim said. "If we don't have someone else to lay in front of him by the week's end, he'll likely push to have Georgia formally charged."

"I don't like the sound of that," Mary said, looking at me. "Couldn't your last...trip...have helped in anyway?"

"What trip?" Jim asked, turning to me. "When did you take a trip? Where did you go?"

"Mary doesn't mean trip as in travel," I said. "It's more metaphorical."

"Yes," Mary said, raising her eyebrow at me. "Metaphorically speaking, was there not something you could've brought back? Surely, there's a new gadget that might help?"

"What are you talking about?" Jim asked, now fully confused and I could see, getting irritated that Mary and I appeared to be speaking in code.

"She's talking nonsense," I said, shooting daggers at Mary. "Ignore her."

Jim tossed down his napkin.

"Enough of this. Keep your little secrets."

"Oh, Jim, don't be like that," I said.

"Like what?" he said, standing up. "Like I need to be a part of the inner circle? Like I need to know what's going on?"

"Jim—" I started.

"No, you'll excuse me," he said. "It's been a long day. Mary, thank you for dinner."

"Jim, don't be like—" I tried again.

"Georgia," he said, looking at me, his face flushed as I visually watched him count silently to ten. "I will see you tomorrow."

Then he turned on his heel and left the room. I listened to the front door shut firmly behind him. Mary tsked.

"And before dessert was served," she said shaking her head.

"Par for the course," I said. "He's been in a snit for days now."

Mary cocked her head as if about to say something but decided against it.

"Let's have our coffee in the salon," she said.

We moved into the living room, little Libby at my feet. Within seconds Seamus was bringing in a tray with big slices of buttery pound cake and a silver server of hot coffee. It was enough to make you think he'd been listening at the door the whole time. After he served us, he retreated, and I fed a part of my cake to Libby.

"It's hard to talk to Jim about some things," I said. "And I'm not even referring to the time travel."

"What kind of things?"

"Well, he can't hear Sam's name mentioned without getting all sulky."

"I'm not surprised."

"It's all so childish," I said. "Winning a big murder case like this means nothing to Jim. It's not like he'll earn praise or new clients from it. He'll carry on doing what he does regardless. But solving this case could really push Sam up the ranks."

Mary's mouth fell open in shock.

"Are you seriously thinking to impress *Sam* by solving this murder?"

Then she put down her coffee with a thunk on the table as if to emphasize her disapproval.

"Well, obviously I have other reasons for solving it," I said defensively.

"Georgia, *Sam arrested you* for the murder."

"Yes, well, Mary, I don't need to tell you that arresting the wrong person for any crime is hardly a way to rise in the ranks."

"I can't believe what I'm hearing. Are you thinking…is it your belief…?" Mary was sputtering she was so flustered now. "Listen to yourself, Georgia! If Sam wasn't impressed with you for solving all those cases last year, what makes you think he'll thank you for this?"

"I have more faith in him than you do."

"Inexplicably, you do," Mary agreed in exasperation.

"If anyone has some explaining to do about his behavior, it's Jim," I said. "He's always stomping out of rooms, like tonight, or giving me the silent treatment. He's becoming unbearable."

"For heaven's sakes, Georgia, can you not understand his frustration?"

"What in the world does he have to be frustrated about?"

Mary threw her hands up in her own expression of frustration.

"It's not complicated," she said. "He's being kept in the

dark and he knows it. He likes you more than you like him. Even us way back here in the Dark Ages of 1924 can see what's happening from his point of view."

"Look," I said, "Jim is a great guy. I see that. And I appreciate that."

"Your problem is that you need to give up on Sam," Mary said. "Even if you could keep who you are a secret, he'll never accept your independent nature. I don't know about Jim, but with Sam it's definite. If he were to find out about the time travel, he'd probably try to get you committed."

"But I love him."

"Said every sad desperate woman ever."

I leaned forward, my eyes blazing, but any retort I might have launched died in my mouth. I turned away and tried to settle my temper.

"Look, just be nicer to poor Jim, would you?" Mary asked.

"Well, he needs to stop acting so protective of me," I snapped. "It's annoying. Where I come from, I actually used to carry a gun. I know how to defend myself."

That wasn't true. But I did take police training and I have shot a lot of paper targets.

"That means nothing in today's world," Mary said. "You are a woman. You are weaker. He is your protector."

"Except he's not."

"Georgia, do you want to be happy? I don't know how they do things in 2024 but nowadays, the man needs to think he's taking care of you. Have men changed so much in a hundred years?"

I shook my head.

"No, they pretty much still feel that way in my time, too."

"Well, there you are then."

21

The next morning, I was slow getting started.

Usually when I feel this way it's a clear indication that I'm discouraged. I refused to admit it, so I went through the motions of washing my breakfast dishes, walking Libby, and dressing for the day. By then, it was late morning. Before his dramatic exit last night, Jim and I had made plans to meet at the Marshall House where they were staying to see which of Celeste Latour's entourage might be available to be interviewed.

What I told Mary last night was true. I really did appreciate all the trouble that Jim was going to for me and I knew it was largely because he was smitten. It wasn't my fault that I couldn't return his feelings and I didn't have the emotional energy at the moment to try and figure out why not. Jim was a great guy. No doubt about that. Loyal, even-tempered, smart and trustworthy. A perfect Golden Retriever Boyfriend for sure. But the heart, as they say, wants what it wants.

I had plenty of time before our arranged meeting time, so I headed for a spot along the way where I could enjoy my lunch. I often came to Bonaventure Cemetery in 2024 to sit and think. Turns out, it's an even better place to sit when you can't hear all the bus tour noises and traffic blaring at you from nearby Highway 80. I sat on a moss-covered stone bench nestled amongst the ancient headstones. All around me, tall oak trees provided dappled shade from the sun, their branches heavy and swaying in the faint breeze. Centuries of footfalls had worn smooth, winding paths through the various plots.

Weathered sculptures and effigies watched silently as I unpacked my tuna fish sandwich with potato chips and an apple from a brown bag. I had plenty of money these days so going out to eat was not a problem. The only real lunch place in the area was the diner and after being hauled out of there in handcuffs, I didn't relish going back quite yet.

I ate my lunch and tried to put a positive spin on my interaction yesterday with Sam. I knew he was a proud man. Even when we were dating and he was supposedly besotted with me, I could see there was a vein of hubris in him that would likely get in the way of him seeing me clearly. I wondered if that was endemic to men back here during this time. I hadn't spotted it yet in Jim but that didn't mean it wasn't there.

Obviously, there weren't the same magazine articles or online posts urging men in the nineteen-twenties to get in touch with their feelings. I'd actually kind of liked Sam's bluster when we were together. It was so unusual from what I was used to. And now that I think of it, Jim is much the same. Must be a nineteen twenties man thing.

After packing up the wrappings from my lunch, I left the cemetery to meet Jim. By the time I got to the Marshall House I was a few minutes late and could see he was waiting for me on the corner. I waved to him, but he didn't wave back. When I reached him, he had a very serious expression on his face.

"What's the matter?" I asked.

"You went to talk to Sam."

I tilted my head to view him.

"How did you know that?" I asked.

I felt a swirl of emotions, ranging from unease to annoyance.

"Why didn't we talk to him together?" he asked.

"What difference does that make?" I asked sharply, now fully deciding on the anger approach to my odd mixture of feelings. "Do you want to hear what I found out or do you want to pout?"

He glanced away from me as if struggling with himself to answer like a normal human being and not a sulking teenager. As he did, it occurred to me that I really hadn't found out anything of value from my conversation with Sam, so Jim's valiant struggle would be for nothing.

"Look," I said, "Sam wouldn't tell me anything about Murphy which isn't that surprising since the police all stick together."

Jim shot me a look.

"You think Sam would lie to cover for Murphy?" he asked.

"I didn't say that," I said. "I'm just saying he wouldn't tell me about him and before you say anything I'm pretty sure he wouldn't tell you either."

Jim stood, his arms folded across his chest, a look of annoyance on his face.

"Let's clear the air, shall we?" I said suddenly.

"Clear the...?"

"What you and I are doing has nothing to do with me and Sam. And even if it did, it would be none of your business. Now you can choose to stay mad and pout or you can put that away and work with me. I need your help, Jim. And if we're going to work together, you need to get over whatever this is."

Somehow, that got through to him. I saw the moment the tension in his face relaxed and he rubbed a hand through his hair.

"Sorry," he said. "You're right."

He smiled somewhat sheepishly at me, and I breathed a sigh of relief. The truth was, I wasn't sure how I would go about doing this without him.

∼

The Marshall House on Broughton Street was built in 1851 and towered above the surrounding buildings on its block. It was seriously steeped in history, had even been used as a Union hospital during the Civil War. Amazingly, it was still used as a hotel in 2024, which I have to say I found very cool.

Jim had gotten the information that all of Celeste's entourage—assistant, husband and agent—were still in Savannah and staying at the Marshall House. I wasn't sure how much longer they would be there, so we wanted to interview the three of them quickly before they all flew away back to Lala Land.

The yellow brick facade of the hotel was decorated with elaborate stone carvings. Large windows overlooked the busy street, their polished panes catching the afternoon sun. When Jim and I stepped inside the hotel I was immediately struck by the refinement of the interior. Gleaming marble floors and intricate wood paneling and crystal chandeliers created a lush, upscale atmosphere. Plush velvet armchairs stood beside an inviting fireplace—the crackling fire set to take the chill off an unseasonably cool day.

We went straight to the registration desk. A twenty-dollar bill slid surreptitiously across the counter had the concierge calling upstairs to Millie Ross's room to tell her she had a delivery downstairs. After that, Jim and I went to the lobby to wait. The afternoon sun filtered through the windows, bathing the space in a soft golden glow.

We didn't wait long. Either Millie Ross doesn't get many messages, or she was expecting someone else. She stepped off the elevator and her eyes darted around the lobby. Her dark hair was styled in loose waves, and her elegant outfit exuded an air of effortless sophistication. She may just be a personal assistant, but clearly, she thought herself on the same rank and level as her recently deceased employer when it came to style. I had to wonder how she could afford her wardrobe on what a personal assistant makes. Her gaze went to the dancing flames in the fireplace and finally to us. She slowed her approach, a worried look now evident in her eyes.

"Miss Ross?" I said with a big smile as I stepped forward to greet her.

She glanced at Jim and for a moment the consternation in her eyes seemed to dissipate. I couldn't blame her. Jim was a serious hunk.

"My name is Georgia Belle," I said as I gently touched her elbow and steered her toward one of those comfy velvet armchairs. "We were hoping to ask you a few questions about your employer Celeste Latour."

"Are...are you the press?" she asked looking again at Jim.

"Not exactly," Jim said as we sat facing one another in a quiet corner of the lobby. "Shall we have tea?"

Without waiting for an answer, he raised a hand at the

concierge who nodded and turned away. I was surprised that Jim thought of it. I'm sure it never would have occurred to me.

I turned back to Millie Ross.

"When are you going back to LA?" I asked.

"Whenever the police say I can," she said with a sigh. "I don't know why the delay. They said they already know who Celeste's killer is."

I nodded sympathetically. Clearly, she did not know she was sitting across from the person whom the police thought of as Celeste's killer.

"Can I ask you, Miss Ross," I said, "where you were the night your employer was killed?"

She started touching her face and blinking rapidly. Something was definitely flustering her. Was it because she wasn't used to lying?

"Why...why are you asking me that?" she said. "I had nothing to do with her death."

"So where were you?"

"Here. In the hotel. I would never come to a speakeasy. They're illegal, you know."

She glanced at Jim as if what she was saying might possibly earn her some points with him.

"I do know that," I said. "But I also know that you have been to a speakeasy before—specifically the Cottonmouth Club—because I saw you there."

She whitened. "Who...who are you?"

"Jim and I—oh, by the way, this is Jim O'Connell."

Millie blushed when I introduced her. Aside from the expensive clothes and carefully cofed hair, Millie was a plain woman with thin lips and a weak chin. I wasn't surprised she was goggling Jim since any woman with eyes would.

"Pleased to meet you," she said breathily to Jim, extending her hand.

He shook it and I think gave her an extra squeeze for good measure before the maître d' showed up with a tray of teacups and cookies and a tall silver teapot. I busied myself with pouring to allow Jim to work his magic.

"This whole experience must have been a terrible ordeal for you," he said to her, scooting a bit closer in his chair.

"It is simply awful!" Millie said. "Truly."

"So, you *were* there that night?" he asked, leaning in close as if in intimate conspiracy with her. "At The Cottonmouth Club?"

She hesitated. "Please don't think ill of me," she said.

I handed her a teacup and a short bread cookie.

"Never," Jim said.

"I don't even know why Miss Latour asked me to come. She always went with the crowd and then as soon as we got in, she never gave me a second look."

"Did you see what happened that night?" Jim asked.

"Not really," she said. "I went to the ladies at one point and when I came back, there was pandemonium."

Boy those restrooms were sure getting a workout when it comes to alibis.

"Is that what you told the police?" Jim asked.

She shook her head and I saw tears glittering in her eyes.

"I lied," she whispered. "I don't know what made me do it."

"You told them you weren't at the Cottonmouth Club, didn't you?" I asked.

She turned to look at me as if surprised I was still there and the look that flashed across her face was one of pure panic. As well she might, I thought with triumph. She'd basically just admitted she had no alibi. Worse, she admitted that she lied about it.

Just like every guilty person ever.

"Look," she said, seeing the look on my face. "I know the police suspect you and I'm sorry about that. Truly. I can't imagine why they would look at you when it's clearly Don Berford who killed her."

"Berford?" Jim said. "What makes you say that?"

"Because of the will," she said, looking from me to Jim and back again.

"Celeste Latour's will?" I asked, feeling my excitement mount. "You've seen it?"

She nodded eagerly.

"I was one of the witnesses. In her will, Celeste leaves everything to Don if she dies first."

22

As soon as we stepped outside of the hotel after our interview with Millie Ross, I felt the day's humidity on my skin. I grant you I'd hoped for a tearful breakdown followed by a confession from Millie. What we got was almost as good—at least as far as gold-standard motives go.

"Surely, Sam knows about this?" I said, turning to Jim. "That the husband stands to inherit? What better motive could there be?"

"I agree," he said. "But keep in mind that Sam definitely does know about it."

I looked at him for a moment and realized he was saying that in spite of this knowledge, Sam was still banking that I was the better suspect. I just couldn't understand him. I just couldn't believe he would turn away from a man standing to inherit millions in favor of a picture of me in my yoga clothes. It just made no sense.

Just then I noticed a familiar figure standing on the edge of the stairs and smoking. Jim turned his head to see where I was looking.

"Do you know him?" he asked.

"It's Celeste's agent, Gerald Tomlinson," I said, feeling a flush of excitement. "Come on, let's have a word."

We hurried over to where the man was standing, rocking back on his heels as he smoked. He wore a three-piece gray flannel suit—much too hot for a typical Savannah summer day—with his fedora set at a jaunty angle. I thought he looked like the quintessential Hollywood schmoozer. He turned when he saw us coming and frowned. Unlike Don Berford, I had no Intel on Tomlinson at all, not even hearsay. I just knew that, as Celeste's agent, he must have been close to her. And I know agents have secrets.

"Excuse me, Mr. Tomlinson," I said. "Might we have a moment of your time?"

Tomlinson's gaze flickered between me and Jim almost as if searching for an escape. He tossed away his cigarette.

"I...I really need to be somewhere," he stammered, taking a step back from our advance.

I fixed him with my most formidable look.

"It'll just take a moment of your time," I said firmly.

The man's eyes switched from my clearly resolute expression to Jim's imposing frame which was effectively blocking any route of escape he might be contemplating.

"Yes, all right," he said. "But make it fast."

"We were wondering if you could tell us where you were the night Celeste Latour was killed," I said.

"What is this?" He glared at us. "I've already spoken to the police."

"So you have an alibi?"

"I don't need to tell you anything."

"Well, we just talked with Millie Ross," Jim said. "And she suggested you were together that night with Miss Latour."

I stifled a grin at this statement since of course Millie had said nothing of the kind, but it got the reaction we were looking for.

"She did?" he said and then recovered quickly. "Look, it's not a crime to be out with friends. And I'll be very upset if you are harassing poor Miss Ross with your baseless accusations. I have half a mind to have a word with the police."

"Miss Ross was actually happy to help," I pointed out. "Especially if our questions lead to the arrest of the person who committed this terrible crime."

Tomlinson flushed again, but this time, it appeared that he wanted to walk back some of his indignation.

"Yes, of course," he said. "We all want that. I would just ask you to be mindful of Miss Ross and her situation."

"What situation is that?" I asked quickly.

But he'd already seen he'd made a misstep.

"None of your business," he said. "She has a lot to deal with is all—what with money and health worries and the way Celeste treated her—like a dog if you want to know. And I'll not have total strangers adding to her troubles."

I'm not sure what Jim made of this outburst, but it made me wonder if there was something going on between Tomlinson and Millie. If there was, it didn't really change anything since an affair between Celeste's agent and her assistant didn't scream *motive* in any way that I could see. It wasn't like she was having the affair with Celeste's husband. Now *that* would have been something worth paying attention to.

"Now I really must go," Tomlinson said in agitation. "Kindly remember what I said about allowing Miss Ross a respectful distance." He turned to leave and then turned back, still flustered. "Look, if you want to talk to someone who hated Celeste, why don't you talk to Janice?"

Both Jim and I looked at each other in surprise.

"Who?" I asked.

"You don't know?" He laughed mirthlessly. "Janice Gruntz. She's Celeste's sister. They look enough alike to be twins. Janice hated her sister because when Celeste set out for Hollywood ten years ago, she never looked back."

"And her sister hated her for that?" Jim asked with a disbelieving frown.

"Well, you tell me," Tomlinson said. "The last time I saw Janice was right here on this very street in front of our hotel not one week ago. The whole world heard her screaming at Celeste."

"Screaming what, exactly?" I asked with excitement. "Do you remember her exact words?"

"Pretty hard to forget," Tomlinson said with a shrug. "She got right in Celeste's face and said '*I wish you were dead, you heartless bitch.*'"

23

Well, that was exciting.

I was astonished that neither Jim nor I even knew about Celeste Latour's sister. After Tomlinson left, I was literally humming with excitement.

A death threat *and* a brand-new suspect possibility! It was a lead made in detective heaven. One thing was for sure, we needed to track down this Janice Gruntz and see what she had to say about where she was at the time of the murder. Unfortunately, as exciting as this new lead was, Jim had a prior engagement he couldn't miss and needed to leave me. I respected the fact that he still had clients—besides me.

In any case, the afternoon light had given way to a rainy evening and frankly I was tired. It wasn't the worst idea in the world for both of us to take a beat to ingest and incubate what we'd learned today.

Jim was confident he could find out Janice Gruntz's address, so we made arrangements to meet up the next day to track her down. I watched him drive off after insisting I didn't need a ride. I had an umbrella, and I wanted the time to think and clear my head. I started down Whitaker Street toward my townhouse. I had just come upon the street across from the diner when I spotted a familiar figure ducking out the side alley door. It was the dishwasher Ruby, probably going for her break.

On impulse, I called to her. "Ruby, wait!"

She turned in surprise and I hurried across the street to join her in the alley between the buildings. Though it was dingy back here—and still raining lightly—after the stifling kitchen Ruby obviously preferred to be outside at least for a moment. I saw the weariness in her eyes from another long shift on her feet.

She gave me a weary smile.

"I remember you," she said. "At the Cottonmouth Club."

"That's right," I said. "I wanted to tell you how sorry I was that you got fired over that incident. That was unfair."

She smiled at me. "Life is unfair."

I pulled out my billfold from my purse and handed her a one-hundred-dollar bill.

"Sometimes it is," I agreed. "So, we need to work harder to tip the scales."

Ruby looked at the money in her hands, her eyes wide.

"I couldn't make this much in six months at the Cottonmouth Club," she said.

"Well, I hope it helps and again, I'm very sorry."

"It weren't your fault, Miss."

"Call me Georgia. May I call you Ruby?"

She nodded.

"It's been hard lately," she said, settling on an upturned food crate and slipping the bill into her shirt pocket. "What with Bert not working."

"Is Bert your husband?"

She nodded.

"He hates being idle." She glanced up at me. "You got a husband, Miss?"

I shook my head.

"Well, men need to feel useful. At least my Bert does."

"We all need to feel useful."

She laughed at that and cocked her head at me.

"I'm not sure I do," she said. "I can't imagine anything better than sitting on a chaise lounge being waited on and doing absolutely nothing."

We both laughed. I nodded at the diner.

"The waitress, Jennie, told me you should be cooking. She says you're great."

"Jennie is kind. But Mr. Johnson don't want no woman cook at the diner."

"His loss," I said as I got to my feet.

Just then I saw Sam walk out of the diner working a toothpick in his mouth.

"Ruby, it was great to talk to you," I said. "But I have to run. I hope you take care of yourself."

"Thank you, Miss. You, too."

After giving her a reassuring smile, I headed straight for Sam. When he saw me coming, I watched his face stiffen which made me slow my advance.

"Georgia," he said coldly and then glanced up at the sky. "You'll get wet. I assume you've gone out without an umbrella."

"As a matter of fact, I have one right here," I said. "Do the rules of getting wet not apply to you?"

I fell into step beside him. I'm not sure where he was heading, probably back to the police station.

"It's different for men," he said with a faint smile.

I felt my heart flutter at the encouragement.

"Look, why don't we sit for a minute?" he said as he pointed to a bench against one of the nearby retail shops.

For Sam to suggest a sit-down visit with me was a definite step forward for us. Or at least that's how I took it. I walked with him to the bench and primly sat down.

"I hope you know how sorry I am about all this," he said sitting down next to me. "You are the last person I would want something like this to happen to."

"You mean being falsely accused of murder?" I said before I could stop myself.

"Georgia, I have evidence."

"Circumstantial evidence."

"Did you hire a lawyer like I suggested?"

"No. I told you. I'm investigating the crime myself. There won't be a trial so there's no need for a lawyer."

"Can you hear yourself?" he said in exasperation. "Georgia, I have to bring you in to be arraigned in five days. Get a lawyer."

"I'm innocent, Sam," I said, suddenly fighting tears.

Why was I having to convince him of this? Does he care for me at all?

"Look," he said, pulling out an envelope from his inside coat pocket.

"This is a copy of the photograph I showed you earlier, the one taken the night Miss Latour was murdered. I don't know how it will help but at least you'll see what we...what the prosecution has against you."

I took the envelope and felt a hollowness develop in my chest. Sam fully intended to go forward to support the prosecution. Giving me the photograph was only to assuage his guilt.

"What about the women who said they heard me threaten Celeste?" I asked.

"They recanted their statements."

I nodded. That was good news, but it was pretty clear how things must have evolved. The women had been in the ladies room the night I was there with Celeste. When the place was raided they probably got scooped up in the raid. I looked at Sam and wondered if he had actively encouraged those women to make their initial statements against me.

Maybe he'd hinted that if they said they'd heard me threaten the victim, he'd go easy on them? Then, as time went by, they decided that testifying in a capital murder trial was worse than being in trouble for going to a speakeasy and they backed out of whatever they said they'd heard. I don't suppose I'll ever know the truth, but the fact that I was even thinking this about Sam was a pretty big red flag. Even I knew that.

"How did Celeste die?" I asked.

He ran a hand through his hair and stood up.

"She was poisoned with a kind of heart medicine that is lethal when taken in quantity," he said.

The fact that he answered me as if he thought I didn't know made me believe that he didn't think I killed her. But in spite of that, he was still going to build a case against me.

I have never felt so hurt or betrayed in my entire life.

"I'm not a bad guy, Georgia," he said as if he could read my mind. "This breaks my heart that this is happening to you."

But even though my brain knew that *he* was the one doing it to me, I still reached out to take his hand. He looked at our clasped hands for a moment and I would've given anything to know what was going through his mind right then. But he seemed to snap out of whatever it was and quickly shook loose from me before turning and walking away without another word.

24

That night was a melancholy one for me.

After taking Libby for a long and very wet walk that evening, I basically took my laptop to bed—which in 1924 basically just served as a word processor and not even one connected to a printer. I wrote a few hundred-word scenarios of the case by which somehow I was found to be proven innocent, after which Sam proposed to me. But, plot twist! In these fictional scenarios, I had the spine to turn him down. I have to say that writing these little exercises should have made me feel better, but tonight they didn't.

The only light on the horizon for me was the fact that Jim and I still had the lead of the victim's sister to follow up in the morning. I swear, if I didn't have that, I'm not sure what I would've done tonight.

The next morning, Jim came to my place early so we could plot out our strategy for questioning Janice. I made coffee and offered him a Pop Tart even though I knew it would probably prompt more questions that it was worth. He sat in my kitchen, feeding pieces of the toaster pastry to

Libby and sipping his coffee. I also knew that as soon as I showed him the photograph that Sam had given me, he'd ask how I got it. And then he'd pout for the rest of the day. But even though I knew that's how he'd react, I decided I couldn't allow that expectation to alter what I needed to do.

Or maybe I just didn't care.

I showed him the photograph. I watched him study it. I knew it captured the scene at the speakeasy in detail. In the foreground, it clearly showed me kneeling on the wooden floorboards in my yoga pants and midriff top. Surrounding me were various patrons, paused in mid-action. To my left, a man leaned casually against the bar, a cigarette dangling from his lips as he gazed vacantly at nothing ahead of him.

In the middle ground scene were several small tables with well-dressed women and gentlemen hunched over their illegal drinks. At one table, three men in sleeve garters and suspenders were talking intently with their heads together, their faces obscured. At another, a solitary woman seemed to smile secretively into her martini. Swirls of cigarette smoke hovered overhead as the wall lamps glowed softly.

"What in the world are you wearing?" Jim asked with a frown, squinting at my yoga clothes.

"Irrelevant," I said brisky.

"Okay. Well, where did you say you got this?"

"Sam gave it to me."

To Jim's credit, I watched him try valiantly to get a grip of himself. He just stared at the photograph, a vein jumping in his forehead, but said nothing.

"Sam said the two women in the ladies room who gave statements against me recanted," I said. "Ruby, the attendant was there, and she heard what really happened but she's black. Will her testimony be deemed credible?"

He frowned.

"You have a very uncharitable view of your fellow man," he said. "Having said that, I wouldn't involve her if we can help it."

He tapped the photograph. "Can I keep this?"

"Sure. What did you find out about the sister?" I asked.

"I have a friend who works in the Municipal Records department downtown. I found out that Celeste Latour changed her name to Latour from the one she was born with—Celeste Gruntz."

"Ugh. I can see why she changed it."

"And from there I was able to find the addresses for both her sister and her mother."

"At least it's something to go on," I said dispiritedly.

"Now, don't start getting all mopey on me. We're far from beat, girl. Chin up."

I couldn't help smiling in the face of his corny optimism. A little less pleasant was the unavoidable comparison of how Sam had treated me not sixteen hours earlier.

∼

Magnolia Manor was a nursing home situated on the outskirts of Savannah, surrounded by the timeless beauty that is South Georgia. The building had an imposing yet graceful structure, its facade crafted from creamy, weathered bricks that had stood the test of time. The place had once been an estate as grand as the long and colorful history it had undoubtedly witnessed. Its exterior was a testament to the elegant architecture of the early twentieth century, evoking a sense of dignity and peace. Perfect for a nineteen twenties old folks' home.

As soon as Jim had found Janice's address, he'd also

found her mother's name and address at Magnolia Manor. When he called there last night to ask a few questions, they were happy to tell him that Janice Gruntz lived in a suburb of Savannah and visited her mother at Magnolia Manor every afternoon after lunchtime. After talking it over with me, we decided it might be less aggressive to approach Janice in a public venue instead of at her home. One thing I've learned the hard way—when it comes to interrogating suspects, degrees matter.

I have to say Magnolia Manor was impressive. White wooden shutters flanked tall, paned windows in front. A wide veranda adorned with ornate, wrought-iron railings wrapped around the front in contrast with the deep green of the rampant ivy climbing the walls.

I tried to remember if I'd ever seen this place in my own time. If I did, it would've made a wonderful bed and breakfast. It occurred to me as we drove up the long winding drive that led to the front of the nursing home that charm was something that didn't often last through the years. In my experience "charm" went very quickly from alluring to dilapidated in the flash of an eye. I shook the depressing thought from my head to concentrate on our mission today.

Jim parked in a gravel lot off to the side of the building. Rocking chairs and benches were scattered on the wide veranda, with a few residents and visitors sitting out enjoying the view of the sprawling lawns which were dotted with ancient oak trees.

"You ready for this?" he asked, glancing at me.

"I was born ready," I said.

But I didn't feel anywhere near as flippant as I sounded. If anything, I was starting to think all our efforts were doomed.

We walked up the steps of the porch and then through a

set of wide, wooden double doors. Above the entrance was a stained-glass transom window which caught the sunlight and cast a kaleidoscope of colors onto the stone steps of the threshold.

Despite the home's age, it was clear that Magnolia Manor was lovingly maintained.

We went to the front desk, gave our names, and were directed to the room of Lillian Gruntz. I was amazed that this was all the security there was. We walked down a carpeted hallway until we came to the door that the receptionist had directed us to and paused. Inside, I could hear a woman's voice. I turned to Jim and motioned for him to stay in the hall while I went in. I tapped on the door and because I knew that privacy was probably something Celeste's mother had given up when she moved in, I just walked in, leaving Jim behind me in the hall.

The room was spacious and filled with natural light, with a dramatic view of the gardens. I wondered if Celeste Latour had paid for this view for her mother. Several large vases of flowers were on various counter tops and on one wall there was a floor to ceiling bookcase filled with books along with a radio. Janice Gruntz was sitting in a straight-backed chair beside her mother who was sitting up in bed.

"Can I help you?" Janice said, her eyes round with surprise to see us.

Janice looked like her sister with the same dark curls and perfect complexion, but she wore no makeup and clearly depended on her hair's natural waves instead of bothering to style it or otherwise enhance it in anyway. Still, except for the fact that her face looked as if it was locked into a permanent grimace, she was attractive.

"Hello, Janice," I said, forgetting that people from this time prefer to be addressed by their titles and last names.

She frowned at my familiar address as if trying to figure out if she knew me.

"My name is Georgia Belle," I said. "I was an acquaintance of your sister." I gestured to all the flowers. "I wanted to give my condolences at your loss."

"Who is it?" the older woman said.

It was clear to see where Janice and Celeste had gotten their looks. Mrs. Gruntz had delicate wrinkles etched into her skin but the high cheekbones, the bow mouth and the lively eyes were all still there despite the years.

"A friend of Cece's," Janice said dismissively before turning back to me. "Thank you, but you are interrupting our visit."

"I won't be long," I said as I walked to the window and looked out. "Wow. What a view. This must have cost a pretty penny."

"What's she saying?" Mrs. Gruntz asked her daughter.

"Excuse me," Janice said, now on her feet, her face flushed with agitation. "I must ask you to leave."

Jim chose that moment to make his entrance and since I could hardly do worse on my own, his presence actually served to shock Janice into a brief silence.

"Hello, all," he said cheerfully before going to the old lady and taking her hand. "How are you, dear? Is everything all right?"

Mrs. Gruntz smiled at him.

"Thank you for asking, young man," she said. "My window keeps sticking. I've told you about it before."

"Not a problem, Mrs. Gruntz," he said. "I'll have it taken care of immediately."

Meanwhile, Janice had recovered sufficiently from the shock of seeing a tall, handsome man in her mother's room.

I even saw her put a hand to her hair as if to check that her curls were still in place.

"I demand to know why you are here," Janice huffed, blushing when Jim turned to cast his baby blues on her.

"Actually," I said, "we're here to talk to you, Janice."

"Me?" she said, fingering the pearls at her throat. "I don't even know you."

I gestured to the elegant furnishings in the small room.

"It certainly looks like Celeste took good care of her beloved mother."

That hit the nail on the head.

Instantly, Janice leaned forward slamming both fists into her thighs.

"Celeste did nothing for our mother!" she hissed. "Okay, sure, she paid a little extra for a room, but did she ever write? Or call? Or visit? No! She abandoned us both without a backward glance."

"I find that hard to believe," I said, hoping to get her more agitated.

In my experience, people stay things they wish they hadn't when they're agitated. Even very careful people.

"Well, you can believe it!" Janice said, folding her arms across her chest. "She had time for everyone but her own mother. Even an old boyfriend! Seeing them together again with him groveling by her side was sickening, I can tell you!"

"Boyfriend?" I asked, snapping my head around to look at her. "Cecelia reconnected with an old boyfriend?"

"If you can call it that," Janice said with disgust. "She made Paddy fawn over her as if nothing had changed. It was humiliating to watch."

I was dumbstruck.

"*Paddy*?" I said. "You don't mean…?"

"Patrick Murphy. She hired him as her bodyguard."

25

Bombshell.

After that explosive bit of Intel, it was pretty clear Jim and I finally had the golden clue we'd been looking for. I didn't even bother asking Janice about the threats that Tomlinson said she'd made against her sister. Jim and I quickly apologized for interrupting their afternoon and got the heck out of there. Both of us were practically thrumming with excitement as we walked back to the car.

"I can't believe Officer Murphy failed to mention the fact of his prior relationship with Celeste Latour when we talked to him," I said.

"I wonder if Bohannon knows about it," Jim said. "We should talk with him."

"No," I said firmly. "Let Sam do his own investigating."

"It's not a contest," Jim said, narrowing his eyes at me. "Whether Sam finds the truth out about Murphy, or we do, it all leads to the same end—your name being cleared."

"Look, I tried talking to him about Murphy before," I said, "and he wasn't open to hearing anything."

"In any case," he said, "it's a good start, but we still need evidence of wrongdoing."

"Agreed. And that starts with destroying the guy's alibi whatever it is. *And* asking him why he didn't tell us he was Cece's old flame."

An hour later, Jim and I were standing on a street in a modest corner of the city, looking at a brick building that had seen better days. Somewhere in this building was a two-bedroom apartment that Officer Patrick Murphy called home. Jim had been able to access the address through a couple of sources at the police department.

We deliberately didn't call first since the best way to catch a suspect off balance is to barge in unannounced. Murphy had lied by omission, and we needed to know the truth behind *why* he lied and how that fit as far as a possible motive. The fact that he'd been overheard threatening Celeste now made all kinds of sense.

Jim knocked firmly on Murphy's door. When it opened, a petite woman with a baby on her hip stood there, looking at us questioningly.

"We're here to speak with Patrick Murphy," I said, momentarily caught off guard by the sweet domestic scene.

The woman called over her shoulder.

"Patrick, sure it's your friends from the station, love!"

Within moments Murphy appeared, rolling up his sleeves where I could see the suds from where he'd been washing dishes. Gone was the dark glare and in its place was a tired yet warm smile.

"You lot again," he said almost affably. "Yes, all right. Come in, come in. Katie, love, why don't you take the wee one upstairs?"

Murphy ushered us into a cozy parlor. A basket of toddler's toys told a different story from the one I'd assumed based on Murphy's looks alone. Jim and I shared a bemused look.

Within moments, Katie hurried back to the living room where we now sat with Murphy.

"Get us some tea, love?" Murphy asked her, his eyes warm when he looked at her.

"And maybe a piece of apple crumble?" she said with a smile before turning to the kitchen.

Looking around, I saw countertops that had been scrubbed to a shine, a well-loved sofa, covered with a patchwork quilt, and a sturdy coffee table stacked with books. The walls were filled with framed family photos capturing moments of laughter and various milestones.

In the corner, a radio cabinet stood out as a prized possession, probably the family's main source of entertainment. In the evenings, I could imagine them all huddled around it to listen to jazz music, radio plays, or the exciting news of Charles Lindbergh's latest aerial feats. Lace curtains that were obviously hand-sewn fluttered in the breeze of an open window, and the clean scent of lye soap, used for everything from washing clothes to scrubbing floors, filled the air.

It was a home brimming with love, stability, and the joy of simple pleasures.

I looked at Jim again and grimaced. We'd misjudged this man. Whatever macho performance he put on by day in fulfillment of his roles as bodyguard or policeman, the real Patrick Murphy was an old softie.

"What can I help you with?" Murphy asked. "I thought I'd told you everything."

"Not quite everything," I said. And then I glanced toward the kitchen and back to Jim. I didn't want to confront Murphy with this while his wife could overhear.

"Me and Katie don't got no secrets," Murphy said. "So, whatever it is, just spill it."

"Okay," I said, dropping my voice in any case. "We were told you knew Celeste Latour before you became her bodyguard."

I didn't have a chance to study Murphy's face because right then Katie came in with a tray of teacups and plates of cake. She bustled about setting the tray down on the coffee table, moving books out of the way. I looked at Murphy, but he was watching his wife's movements. After pouring our tea, she sat down next to him.

"I know all about Celeste Latour," she said to us. "And who she was before she was Celeste Latour."

"You heard that me and Cece used to walk out together, right?" Murphy asked me.

I nodded.

"In school," he said. "A hundred years ago. But yeah, we were sweethearts back then. Hard to imagine, innit?"

His wife gently slapped his arm in admonishment.

"Any girl would be lucky to have you, Paddy," she said. "I was."

"Can I ask how you got the job of guarding her?" I asked.

He shrugged.

"I didn't ask for it, if that's what you're thinking. It was offered to me by her agent. Me and a bunch of us down at the station, mind. You know, as a way to make extra money."

"Was that uncomfortable for you?" Jim asked.

Murphy laughed.

"Not for *me*. Cece liked to pretend she didn't remember none of when we were together. Which was fine. She was all different now. Lived in Hollywood. I wouldn't be surprised if she didn't remember nothing from when she grew up here."

"You were overheard threatening her," I said, glancing at Katie who immediately frowned.

"Threatening her?" Murphy said, his tone disbelieving. "What was I supposed to have said?"

"That you would fix her wagon," Jim said.

Both Murphy and Katie stopped and looked at each other and then burst into laughter. Katie dried her tears with the corner of her apron.

"You'll have to excuse us," she said. "But that's what we say to the kiddies all the time. Don't we, Paddy?"

Murphy nodded.

"We got three. The older two are in school but they get up to some hijinks, I'll tell you."

"So was Celeste Latour getting up to some hijinks?" I asked.

Murphy shook his head.

"Sure, no, she wasn't that way. Always a lady was Cece. I know what day you're talking about. Her agent had just given her a script for a part where she was to play the mother. That's a come down for her, ya see?"

Jim and I both nodded, waiting for the full explanation.

"So she takes the script and starts going on about how it's over for her and she's an old crone—"

"If you can imagine!" Katie interjected. "Celeste Latour an old crone! She's not forty years old!"

Murphy grinned ruefully.

"She wasn't listening to her husband," he said, "and since it was her agent who brought her the script, she shouldn't have been listening to him anyway, but she was going down further and further into this…depression, like."

"And this happened at the Cottonmouth Club?" I asked.

"It did. She was drinking like it was her last day on earth. If she'd been my wife I'd have cut her off, but I only worked for her so all I could do was jolly her up, like."

"Paddy said she even told him she wanted to kill herself!" Katie said, shaking her head sadly.

"That's when I thought I ought to get a little tough with her," Murphy admitted. "I told her under no circumstances was she to say things like that. And if she tried, I'd fix her wagon but good."

He turned to look at his wife.

"It made her laugh," he said. "And then she said something like, *you always could make me laugh, Paddy*."

"I wanted to tell her, *hands off, honey*," Katie said with a grin as she hugged her husband's arm. "*He's mine.*"

They kissed briefly and then remembering they had an audience pulled apart in embarrassment. Murphy addressed me in all seriousness.

"I didn't know if Cece was really thinking of hurting herself and I knew she wasn't going to listen to me. Heck, she was heading back to LA in a few days. But I was worried about her. That horse's ass of a husband of hers was more of a prima donna than she was. She needed somebody to look out for her."

"All that money," Katie said wistfully. "And all those fans and fame. And yet when it came down to it, nobody really knew her or loved her."

Murphy squeezed his wife's knee, and I thought I saw something pass across his face that revealed how grateful he was for how things had turned out.

A few minutes and a couple of delicious slices of apple crumble cake later, Jim and I said goodbye to the pair and headed back up the road. I didn't need to do too much conferring with Jim on the walk back to confirm what we both felt. The look on Murphy's face when he looked at Katie was not feigned. He wasn't in love with Celeste if he ever had been.

He only pitied her for the life she had made.

26

After leaving Murphy's neighborhood, Jim and I split up for the rest of the day. We were going to hit the Cottonmouth Club again tonight to see who had been there the night of the murder to see who could be questioned. One of the waitresses had mentioned a bartender who was off duty when we went before.

That afternoon I was supposed to be napping to get ready for our night of intense interviewing, but I found myself getting more and more discouraged about the case and my chances of my solving it. Crossing Murphy off my list had significantly depleted my list of suspects—as in all of them, besides possibly Janice. I had one last trick up my sleeve, but I was seriously hoping I wouldn't have to use it. Just thinking about going back to 2024 so soon after my last trip—which was what my backup plan entailed—turned my stomach.

I ate a pot of Ramon noodles for dinner—making them for the first time not in a microwave—and then took Libby for a long walk. The streets were still glistening with the afternoon rain. I knew I should be resting, not logging in steps, but I was just too restless and disheartened to nap.

Libby and I walked to Crawford Square, a few blocks from my townhouse, where I found a dry spot on a bench and let her sniff some bushes while I sat and looked out over the landscaping. I think it was the emotional rollercoaster today of believing I'd found a viable suspect only to have to remove him from my list that got to me the most. And honestly, Murphy had never been a great candidate. I'd already suspected that the mode of killing—poison—wasn't his style. And now his motive was gone, too.

I looked around the small square and took in a long breath. This square was an historic place in my time and was still used frequently in 1924. There was an old-fashioned water cistern in the center of the square—in lieu of a fountain, I guess—to help fight fires should the need arise. And since this was Savannah, the need was always arising.

As I sat there, I couldn't help but wonder what Sam was doing tonight. Since as far as he was concerned, he'd already solved this case, I wondered if he was at home listening to a ball game on the radio? Or was he out on a date? I felt a wave of wistfulness knowing that I couldn't call him and talk to him.

One thing I knew if I knew anything: he didn't want to hear from me.

How had I ever thought he'd be open to getting back together? What part of his personality or this time period or his past behavior had led me to think there was a chance of that? And because I'd stupidly refused to accept it when he turned away from me, now I was faced with enduring all the pain of feeling hurt and broken-hearted all over again. And of course, add to that the knowledge that it was all my own fault.

Libby gave a sharp yap and I realized I'd been lost in my own unhappy little world for a while now and she'd been trying to get my attention. It was getting dark, and we needed to be getting back home.

∾

Jim came by to pick me up around nine o'clock. I'd made an effort to dress for the part tonight. I wore a shimmering gown of silver lamé which clung nicely to my curves, with a drop waist and beaded fringe that swished enticingly at the knees. Black silk gloves, a feathered boa and matching headband completed the look. I felt somewhat ridiculous, as I always do when I dress up for this time period, but this was the costume one wore to the Cottonmouth Club and to wear anything else would make me much too conspicuous.

Jim on the other hand looked the total opposite of ridiculous. He showed up at my door in a pinstripe suit with the jacket fitted to show off his broad shoulders and a fedora tipped at a rakish angle over one eye. I'm pretty sure my mouth dropped open when I opened the door and saw him. There's something about hanging with someone in everyday clothes and then seeing them dressed up that can really fluster you. Or maybe that's just me. Jim went from my guy pal to Clark Gable in the time it took to open my front door and I'm not sure I was ready for it.

Correction: I wasn't ready for it.

In any case, we got over any awkwardness by climbing into his Model T and heading out into the night. We hadn't had much time to debrief on our visit with Murphy this afternoon, but it was clear we were both on the same page as far as he was concerned. He'd dropped way down our very short list of suspects. Gut instinct and a detective's natural intuition about a person count for a lot in these cases and I was glad to see that Jim wasn't tempted to dismiss my assessment as women's intuition. In fact, he felt the same way, which was that Murphy had a happy life now and nothing about the shallow superficial way that his old love had turned out had felt to him like anything but a bullet dodged.

The fact that our lead—so gorgeously viable just a few hours earlier—had disintegrated after interviewing Murphy in his home did nothing but increase the slowly building discouragement we were both feeling about the investigation. Even worse, we were now officially sitting on a ticking time bomb. Any time now, Sam would be forced to bring me in to be formally arraigned for Celeste's murder. If I didn't have someone else to lay before him, I was going to be tried for murder.

The minute Jim and I stepped into the Cottonmouth Club, a wall of sound and heat enveloped us. A fog of hazy cigarette smoke hung over the dance floor which was packed with bodies in motion to the lively band. Colorful costumes swirled together passionately under the lights. I craned my neck to see if there was anyone I recognized.

Along the walls, plush booths and loveseats cradled couples in deep conversation. I noticed again a couple of doors that I imagined led to smaller rooms for more intimate drinking parties, or perhaps card games. Waiters moved smoothly among the throng with loaded trays of drinks.

I felt Jim take my elbow and sparks seemed to radiate from his touch. I turned to look and saw he was watching the bar where none other than Don Berford was standing nursing a drink. We immediately moved in that direction.

Berford, a tall man with a rough, unshaven jaw and a permanent scowl etched into his features, looked more like he belonged in a back alley doing drug deals than dressed in a seersucker suit sitting in an expensive speakeasy. When we'd first spotted him, he seemed to be staring intently into his drink, but his shoulders stiffened as soon as he saw us coming. The noise of conversations and the raucous jazz music seemed to intensify around us as he locked eyes with us. Here I go with gut intuition again, I thought. Or maybe I'm just a really good judge of sociopaths. But there was something dangerous in Berford's gaze. Whether it was the drink or just the kind of man he was, he looked like someone itching for a fight.

"Don Berford?" I said pleasantly—but loudly—over the noise of the music.

"Who wants to know?" he said belligerently.

"Let's just say someone who overheard you planning to kill your wife," I said.

I saw the fury building in his face as he turned to me, his jaw clenched tightly.

"You didn't hear anything," he said.

At this close range, I could smell the alcoholic fumes pouring off him.

"Maybe you can explain what I did hear," I said reasonably. "You said '*I want to be free. How do I get out of this?*' Sounds like a threat to me—"

Just then, with an explosive grunt, Berford shoved me hard, sending me backward into Jim's arms. Berford got to his feet, knocking into a table and advancing on us, his eyes blazing. Jim deftly spun me out of the way just as Berford swung. Jim blocked the attack with his forearm before plowing his fist into Berford's unprotected midriff.

Berford groaned and bent over before going down on one knee.

"Look, man," Jim said, reaching out to help the big man up. "We just want to—"

But Berford was too far gone to listen. He lurched at Jim with a guttural scream. Jim easily deflected the attack and wrestled him under control, twisting his arm behind his back. The speakeasy erupted into chaos with patrons crying out in alarm as Berford continued to thrash in Jim's iron grip. It was clear he was not going to go down without a fight.

27

After that, things disintegrated pretty quickly.

A bouncer materialized from out of nowhere and escorted all three of us out of the club. Berford stormed off in a huff cussing threats at us the whole way. Because we'd gotten precisely nothing from him before things went sideways, the drive back to my place was dispiriting to say the least. Jim didn't even have the energy to suggest this was just a little setback. Nor did we make plans to get together tomorrow. I think we both knew we needed a break. A part of me thought we needed a break because I needed to come to terms with the fact that we'd failed, and that it was time for my drastic and much dreaded Plan B.

After Jim dropped me off, he waited until I climbed the steps to the porch before driving away. If he'd waited, he would've seen the shadow sitting on the corner of my porch appear out of the darkness to confront me as I started to put the key in the lock on my front door.

"I can't even believe what you are doing," the voice said, low and menacing.

I shrieked and lashed out with my keys, aiming for his

eyes as I'd been taught in self-defense classes. Thankfully, Sam was able to block the motion before I'd succeeded in seriously injuring him.

"What the hell, Georgia!?" he yelped as he twisted the keys out of my hands.

All the noise we were making set off Libby who was now howling and barking as if a platoon of commandoes had landed at the front gate. I felt an unexpected combination of relief that I wasn't about to be assaulted on my own front porch, and fury for having had the daylights scared out of me.

"What are you doing sneaking around my porch?" I snapped at him as I grabbed my keys back and jabbed them into the door lock.

I opened the door just as Libby charged out, heading straight for Sam and stopping just short of sinking her tiny little canines into his ankle.

"It's all right, Libby," I said, leaning down to scoop her up.

I turned to face Sam, not inclined to let him in. I admit I'm a fool but even I have moments of clarity.

"I left the station tonight," Sam said, "just as the husband of my murder victim called to make an assault charge against Jim O'Connell."

Sam turned to indicate the street where he'd no doubt watched Jim drive off.

"That was self-defense," I said. "The pig attacked me."

To Sam's credit, that information took a bit of the wind out of his sails. But still, Jim had been the white knight to come to my aid, not Sam, and regardless of how he felt about me right now, it was still going to take a while before he could be totally accepting about that.

"Why were you even there?" he demanded.

"At the speakeasy? Because I'm pretty sure Mr. Berford didn't admit to being there the night of the murder," I said pointedly. "And we both know he had the best motive of all for killing Celeste."

"That is not the point," Sam said between gritted teeth. "Don Berford is the husband of the victim of a major crime, and you are my prime suspect for that crime. Are you *asking* me to take you back into custody?"

"So it's against the law for me to defend myself against bodily attack?" I asked, crossing my arms.

He frowned.

"You are seriously telling me that Berford attacked you?"

"He did! Yes!"

Sam frowned as if considering this.

"So is Berford filing charges against Jim?" I asked.

"I don't know. He was mad. But he was also drunk. He might decide not to when he calms down."

"He also might decide not to once witnesses at the Cottonmouth Club tell what really happened tonight," I said. "He attacked a woman. In a speakeasy."

"Your argument sounds much less convincing when you mention the speakeasy," Sam said sharply. "Most people would think a woman who went to that kind of place got what she deserved."

"Is that what you believe?" I asked, holding his gaze with mine.

"Of course not. Don't twist my words."

"I am fighting to stay out of prison," I said biting off every word in my frustration. "I went to a speakeasy to talk to anyone who might help me mount a defense. I wasn't there to go dancing."

He looked at my dress and raised an eyebrow.

"What was I going to do?" I said, raising my voice, "show up in overalls?"

"Look," he said, using his hands in a placating gesture, especially since I could tell my voice was carrying down the quiet street. "Let's just leave it for tonight, shall we? Tell O'Connell he'll need to come by the station to answer the charge."

"If there is one," I said in a huff.

"Just tell him," he said. "And Georgia?"

I turned to look at him.

"If you could be a little more circumspect? Please?"

As I watched him go, I wanted to ask him how *circumspect* he'd be if *his* life was hanging in the balance. But I was starting to think that Sam didn't really see things from other people's points of view. As I watched him walk down the sidewalk to his car, the realization of his lack of real feeling for me hit me like a hammer to the forehead. Sometimes that's the way it has to be for the truth to really sink in. At least with me.

After that, I put Libby on her leash and walked down to Mary's townhouse. Regardless of how many people Jim and I spoke to, I was stalled in the investigation. Something needed to happen, and I couldn't do that here. With my head down and my pace a veritable trudge even with Libby pulling on her leash, it was late by the time I reached Mary's house. Her butler Seamus answered the door in his shirtsleeves, reminding me that I was knocking on doors well past the socially accepted time to be doing that. He looked at me as if I were an apparition, so dramatically startled was he to see me there. Honestly, I do think if butlering doesn't work out for him, he should try the stage. He's got a definite flair for the dramatic. Fortunately, Mary appeared from behind him.

"Thank you, Seamus," she said. "I'll handle this."

She ushered me and Libby inside where we stood in the foyer.

"What is going on?" she asked.

I handed her the leash.

"I have to go away for a little bit," I said.

Instantly Mary began wringing her hands.

"Georgia, no! You just came back!"

"I know, but I have to. I'm not getting anywhere here trying to prove my innocence."

"What proof do you think you'll find in 2024?"

We walked into her salon, and I saw that Roomba was in its charging station. Mary had used the robot almost daily since I'd given it to her. Cook appeared in the doorway and gave the machine a dirty look before addressing her mistress.

"Will you want tea?"

"No thank you, Lenore," Mary said with a strained smile. "Go to bed."

The cook disappeared and Mary turned back to me, her face creased in a deep frown. Libby settled down at my feet, her head on her paws.

"They'll have a record of the murder case somewhere in the city or media archives," I said in a low voice. "Celeste Latour was famous. I'll be able to find the case and see what the police had to solve the case in 1924."

"But what good will that do? You can't lay a 2024 newspaper in front of Sam! He'll think it's a fake!"

"I don't have to bring the actual paper back. The facts of the story will point me in the direction of the evidence that cleared me. I just need to come back and locate the same evidence during this time. Trust me, it'll be a shortcut to proving my innocence."

"Will it be worth the five years it'll chop off your life?"

"I'll be fast."

"Isn't that the very thing you said caused the aging jump before?"

I hadn't realized that Mary was listening to me as closely as she obviously had been. But I knew she was worried about me. And I couldn't fault her for that.

"I don't have any other ideas, Mary."

She looked at me solemnly.

"You could stay in 2024," she said.

"I won't."

"Don't say that. You will if it's for the best. I assume you're not wanted for murder in 2024?"

"I won't," I repeated, shaking my head. "I can't leave and have Sam believe I was guilty of this."

"What Sam believes is irrelevant, Georgia," Mary said in frustration. "When will you get that through your thick skull? Nothing you do will make a difference to how he feels about you."

"I don't care," I said. "I can't have him thinking I murdered someone."

"But he *does* think that," she said in exasperation. "Ask yourself, would a real friend think it of you?"

We'd had this argument so many times before.

"Mary, Sam has evidence he can't ignore. I don't blame him for that."

"Well, maybe you should."

"I'll be gone a little longer this time," I said. "I need to do the research and also see my mother. I haven't seen her in nearly three months—nor spoken to her in all that time."

"Yes, yes, of course, you must go," Mary said in resignation.

I stood up.

"I know I'm doing the right thing," I said. "And coming back is the right thing, too."

I knelt and gave Libby a cuddle.

"Be a good girl, Libster. I'll be home soon."

After that, Mary walked me to the door.

"Whether you come back or not," she said as we stood at the door, "it's time for you to decide which timeline you want to live in before you're an old woman at thirty. You already look like you're in your forties. Too much more, and you'll age yourself right out of the husband market. At least in 1924."

I laughed in spite of myself and gave Mary a long hug before turning and hurrying off the steps of her front porch and into my uncertain future.

28

The trip back was nothing short of gut-wrenching. Neither roller coaster nor walk in the park, it was like falling off a cliff while my skin was being flayed off me.

Not wonderful.

I once more ended up some place other than my apartment. I'd given this some thought since last time, and I decided that whatever supernatural being had his hand on the throttle for this time travel process must not consider my shabby little apartment in 2024 truly my home. That's my theory.

In any event, I landed with a bone-jarring thud in a ditch next to the construction site for yet another Publix supermarket being built a few blocks from my apartment. I took the time to vomit up my hasty dinner of Ramen noodles and then climbed out of the ditch, my head aching like ten hangovers. It was late evening—as it had been back in 1924—and by the time I made it to my front door I was done. It was all I could do to put the code into the lock to get the door open before stumbling to my bed where I fell instantly asleep for the next twelve hours.

I woke up and turned on my Keurig coffeemaker and found a bagel in the freezer that I popped in the toaster, amazed at how easy life was compared to how I live back in 1924. It wasn't just the actual time traveling which I found so discombobulating, but even just being in this time after a few weeks "back there" was disorienting. I seemed to be in a constant state of unbalance.

The first thing I did after breakfast was to plug in my cellphone which I'd forgotten to do the day before when I collapsed into bed. I tried to get the weather from Alexa and instantly realized I had no WIFI access—I suppose I must have missed that payment. I have to say that I'd gotten out of the habit of looking at my cellphone as a receptacle for messages of any kind so after I plugged it in on the kitchen counter, I grabbed a bottle of water and headed out the door without checking for any messages that might have been sent while I was "gone."

My first stop was the Internet cafe on the corner of Bull Street and East Anderson. I'd stashed some of the cash I'd gotten from my last banking visit to 2024 in the apartment and paid for an hour of computer time—my own laptop was still back in 1924—and high bandwidth Internet access. The first thing I did was Google *Celeste Latour murder.*

All the media stories I found on the 1924 murder of the famous Hollywood star Celeste Latour revealed the killer to be a mysterious young woman with no family and no past who was arrested, charged and tried for the sensational murder. I read the online stories, one after the other, with my hand on the mouse shaking and my stomach lurching up into my throat.

Savannah Woman Sentenced to Death Row

(Savannah, GA) - In a highly publicized trial, local resident Georgia Belle was found guilty of first-degree murder for the poisoning death of Hollywood socialite and screen star Celeste Latour.

Latour's body was found in the infamous night club The Cottonmouth Club on the night of April 5, 1924.

Prosecutors argued that Belle was overheard fighting with Latour the night the actress was murdered. They presented evidence that showed beyond a shadow of doubt that Belle procured the same type of poison used in the killing. Despite Belle's claims of innocence, the jury deliberated for just two hours before returning a guilty verdict. Superior Court Judge Robert Franklin sentenced Belle to death by hanging.

My stomach roiling, I continued searching for articles, my hands trembling on the keyboard as I found another more recent article, dated 1944.

Movie Star Killer Dies on Death Row

(Savannah, GA) Georgia Belle, a prisoner at Lowell Correctional Facility, was found unresponsive in her cell late yesterday evening. Authorities are currently investigating the circumstances surrounding the death but believe that Belle died of natural causes. Belle had lived on death row at the correctional facility for twenty years. At fifty-six years of age, Belle continued to deny her involvement in the high-profile murder of Celeste Latour, a movie star who had been visiting the Savannah area with her husband and entourage.

The Latour murder gripped headlines nationwide for many years. While justice has seen Belle pay for her crime with a lifetime behind bars, this tragic tale seems to have at last come to its close.

I sat and stared at the archived online news story and then dove deeper and searched for any stories I could find—but every one of them told the same story. By the time my paid-for Internet time was up and my searching had led over and over to the same terrible end, I sat back in my chair shaken and sickened.

This meant that Celeste Latour's killer was never found. If I returned to 1924 and I cannot change this narrative, I will die in prison. All I could do was sit there and shake my head in denial and horror. This was my Plan B! I'd been so sure I'd walk away with my defense all wrapped up. Instead, I was so freaked out I could barely manage to swallow or control my breathing. I don't know what I'd been hoping for. I should have known that if I didn't find the real killer, this was the way things were going to play out.

And then it hit me.

I didn't have to go back. In fact, it would be madness to go back. My stomach flipped at the realization. I got up and left the café and just walked, not seeing where I was going and not caring. It was early fall, and the weather was nice, not too hot. I walked without seeing where I was going until I realized I was standing in front of the Colonial Park Cemetery. Tears came to my eyes as I stared at it, realizing how many times I'd gotten succor and comfort sitting in this peaceful oasis. Created in 1789, the cemetery was basically an asphalt park with a pond, a greenhouse, and a winding walkway through a bunch of flowers and trees. And of course, lots of headstones. Like the Marshall Hotel and so many other buildings in Savannah, it has features dating back to the Civil War such as the surrounding iron fence which separated the living from the dead. Spanish moss hung in tatters from the massive oaks towering over the graves.

Looking across the old tombstones, most worn smooth by the decades and decades of wind, I could see how they all leaned and tilted in uneven rows. I sat down and tried to take stock of where I was and what I needed to do. It was pretty clear that staying in 2024—safe and sound and not dying on death row was my obvious and best option. And then I thought of Mary and Sam and even Jim. Not that any of them were enough on their own to make me stay with an axe hanging over my head. I knew that Mary would understand. But even so, I should at least tell her what was happening.

I rubbed a hand across my face. The very thought of going back to say goodbye twisted me into knots. I wanted desperately to seem them all again—even little Libby—but I hated the thought of it. Worse than going back to say goodbye was letting Mary wonder what had happened to me. As I sat there in the cemetery, I thought of my beautiful townhouse I'd spent so much effort and time fixing up.

One thing was for sure, I'd never be able to walk down East Peter's Street without weeping. I knew Mary would take good care of Libby. I thought about Sam and wondered if, except for losing his prime suspect, he'd even care that I disappeared. He'd probably get in trouble for letting me loose on bond. I knew he must have vouched for me somehow. And now I would be letting him down. Maybe he'd even suffer a demotion because of it? Then I realized all the money that Mary would be on the hook for because she'd posted my exorbitant bond.

My vision blurred as I fought to keep the tears at bay. I am sure I have never been this low, this devastated by anything in my life, and I wasn't entirely sure I was strong enough to withstand it. I felt a sudden, visceral urge to talk to my mother and felt in my bag, looking for my phone to call her when I realized I'd left it back at my apartment. It should be fully charged by now. I got up and made my way out of the cemetery and slowly walked home, each footfall feeling like my shoes were encased in cement.

When I turned the last corner toward my apartment, I was startled to see a familiar form waiting on my front stoop.

"Jazz?" I said as I came closer.

She had been studying her phone but looked up when I called her name, her face instantly awash in anguish. I instantly stopped walking.

"Where have you been, Georgia?" Jazz asked, her voice full of the threat of tears.

"What's happened?" I asked in a near whisper.

"Oh, sweetie," she said, the tears coming freely now. "I am so sorry."

29

The morning sun trapped by the dense canopy of oak trees lining West Charlton Street beat down relentlessly on Jim as he walked down the street. It wasn't yet noon and already a sheen of sweat beaded on his forehead as he walked. A horse-drawn cart rumbled by its driver calling out greetings to pedestrians. Traffic wasn't busy in this residential section of town. On many of the porches he passed, he spotted women fanning themselves while sipping tea and watching the world walk or drive by.

A nice life, he thought. A quiet life.

He'd called Georgia twice this morning but there was no answer. He knew she was discouraged by their series of dead-end interviews, but he'd hoped to reassure her this morning that they were far from beat. But the truth was, he was worried.

That was partially the reason he'd decided to take his midmorning stroll down East Peter's Street to check on her. He couldn't imagine her being home and *not* answering her phone but perhaps she was still in bed. That didn't seem to correspond with what he thought he knew about her, but then she was not quite herself these days.

A few yards down the sidewalk he spotted Mary Thompson walking Georgia's dog. Jim frowned and quickened his pace.

Is Georgia out of town?

He waved at Mary and watched her stop, seemingly unsure for a moment until she recognized him. She didn't immediately smile at him though, which told Jim she wasn't pleased to see him.

"Good morning, Mary," he said as he joined her and knelt to ruffle Libby's ears. "I see she's got you on dog patrol this morning."

"Good morning, Jim," Mary said, glancing around.

It almost seemed to Jim as if Mary was looking for an escape. He straightened up.

"How are you this morning?" he asked, crossing his arms.

In her gauzy floral summer dress, Mary looked like she had not a care in the world as she walked down the street. Jim had always thought Mary was a fine-looking woman and she was still young enough to find a husband. He didn't know why she didn't have a string of beaus lining up around the block.

"Very well, thank you," she said. "And yourself?"

"Well enough," he said. "So where is she? Out of town again?"

"Yes," Mary said taking a step as if to walk past him on the sidewalk. "A little weekend visit, I believe."

"Where?" he asked.

He hated to be so blunt. He knew that Mary would bend over backwards to observe the rules of social courtesies and he hated to use that tendency against her. But now that he knew that the reason Georgia wasn't answering her phone was because she wasn't home, he needed to know why she would leave in the middle of their investigation.

"Oh, to her mother's home in Jacksonville, I believe," Mary said.

It was that *I believe*, that told Jim she was lying. To her credit, Mary wasn't a natural liar.

"Did she tell you about our altercation last night at the speakeasy?" he asked.

"Oh?" Mary asked. "No, she didn't mention it."

"I didn't think at the time that it had upset her so much," he prompted.

"Well, it must not have," Mary said evasively. "Because she never said anything to me about it."

Jim narrowed his eyes.

"So why did she leave? Was it something I did?"

Mary let out an exasperated sound and looked at him for the first time.

"Georgia didn't leave because of anything you did or said, Jim."

"But you won't tell me where she went."

"I thought I just did." Then her shoulders sagged in defeat. "I'm not at liberty to share that with you, Jim. I'm sorry."

"Does her leaving have to do with Sam?"

The question was out of his mouth before he knew he was going to ask it. He instantly regretted it. Mary looked at him with pity.

"Jim, she's working through all that."

"Because she's still in love with him?"

Mary opened her mouth as if to say something and then thought better of it.

"He's not right for her," he said, feeling the anger

building up inside him. "He won't even defend her when she needs it."

From the expression on her face, he could tell Mary agreed with him.

"Georgia can be blind to some things," she said.

"She isn't from these parts, is she?" he asked.

"What has she told you?"

"Almost nothing."

"Well, then, Jim, I really do think that's a conversation the two of you need to have. Now if you'll excuse me, I need to get home."

Jim watched Mary turn and walk back the way she came and felt momentarily guilty for how he had ambushed her. Clearly, she was fond of him, but she wouldn't tell him what he wanted to hear—especially if it wasn't true. Instead, she had done everything she could to spare his feelings. He turned back toward his own neighborhood. It was a long walk, but he found he needed the time to think.

30

The Old Pink House bar was in an historic building downtown with thick brick walls and towering windows that looked out onto the old-fashioned cobblestone street in front of it. Tourists loved it, I thought as I glanced out the window. For them it was like taking a step into the distant past.

The main floor of the bar had high ceilings with exposed wooden beams and an industrial-chic vibe. Flatscreen TVs lined the walls playing various sports games. The long marble bar where Jazz and I sat was crowded with locals enjoying craft cocktails. Behind the bar, a massive selection of bourbons and specialty liquors glowed from warm amber lights. A wall of beers from local breweries kept patrons stocked. It was amazing to think how all of this was against the law back in 1924. I signaled to the bartender to bring me another vodka tonic.

I didn't want to go back to my apartment. I didn't want to pick up my phone and see the series of text and voice mail messages that had been left for me. Instead, I sat at the bar with Jazz who watched me with concern and helplessness.

Three days ago, when nobody could reach me to notify me of my mother's unexpected death at Saint Joseph's Hospital, Jazz had gone to my apartment building in search of me. She'd left a note on the door which must have blown away. And she'd asked all of my neighbors to call her if they noticed I'd returned. One of my neighbors had called her this morning.

"How are you doing, sweetie?" she asked in a soft voice.

I turned to her, stunned and gutted. She'd tried to tell me in as gentle way as she could, and I know she was trying to imagine where in the world I'd been instead of here when my mother died. Right after she told me the terrible news, she handed me her phone and I was able to talk to my mother's physician. I think I was only hearing one out of every twenty words the man said. My brain was buzzing in overtime, mostly trying to refuse the facts that everyone was setting before me.

Mom had gone in for routine tests related to her history of heart disease. The *routine tests* had included scans that carried more risk for someone with heart disease. The postmortem hadn't been finished yet, but it appeared that she had collapsed unexpectedly and died due to an aneurysm.

"They said no one could've predicted it," Jazz was saying, wringing her hands and looking at me fretfully.

It occurred to me that she might be acting guilty on my behalf. Which made no sense.

Because the only one who was guilty was me.

"Where were you, Georgia?" she asked softly. "We tried to reach you. I looked everywhere."

I nodded. What did it matter now? I certainly wasn't going to tell Jazz what I'd told my mother—what I'd lied to her—that I was undercover and incommunicado. Jazz had worked with me in Dispatch. She'd know it was a lie. But I couldn't tell her the truth either. So, what did it matter?

"I was nowhere," I said miserably.

Somehow that felt more like the truth than anything else I could have said. I thought of my mother's face the last time I'd seen her. Smiling. Of course, she was always smiling. I would give everything I have—even my very life—to hear her voice one last time. A chance to say goodbye and to thank her for all she did for me. To tell her how much I loved her.

The same feeling I'd been trying so hard to bury came roaring back and embedded itself like an icepick in my gut: *I could have seen her the last time I was in 2024. But I'd chosen not to.*

I'll have to live with that for the rest of my life. If I can. Losing her like this was worse than a sudden car accident where she was just snatched from me—as horrible as that would've been. Because she'd reached out to me to try to see me, and I'd put her off, I'd walked away from my one chance to see her one last time. I wasn't sure if I was ever going to be able to forgive myself for that. It almost felt as if I was the one who killed her.

I ordered another drink, but Jazz put a hand on mine to stop me. She removed her hand as if she'd changed her mind, but it gave me a moment to think.

She's right. I don't deserve to anesthetize myself from this pain. I deserve to feel every bit of it.

I looked around the bar—so modern with nobody afraid of the police busting in any minute to slap the glass of beer out of their hands. It was so easy to live here with its convenience foods, its convenience life. And yet this was the world where I'd failed my mother.

The next thought hit me hard: *in 1924 my mother hasn't been born yet. The possibility of her still exists.*

The notion came to me like a razor cutting through flesh, and just as painful. Here was my back up plan after all. My Plan B. It was suddenly as clear as anything to me.

I'd rather go to prison than live a free woman in 2024 without my mom.

Correction.

I *deserve* to go to prison and die on death row for how I'd failed her.

I was going back.

31

The neighborhood surrounding Jim's apartment was in a section of town that had been built after World War I. The architecture of the buildings, which appealed to Jim, was basically utilitarian with faded brick facades and front stoops worn by the tread of countless boots. Fire escapes zigzagged across the exteriors instead of being hidden in the back as they would be in the nicer neighborhoods. These buildings bore the soot and imprint of an industrial city, with laundry strung between windows, fluttering like flags against a hazy sky. No pretensions. As honest as the day and just about as ugly.

As he made his way to his apartment building, the scent of fresh bread, cured meats, and coal smoke filled the air. The economic disparity from Mary and Georgia's neighborhood and this one was glaringly evident. While some buildings on the street showed signs of upkeep, others like the one housing Jim's apartment were in various states of disrepair with boarded-up windows and the occasional condemned notice plastered on the door.

He nodded at a tall mixed-race man standing on the

corner smoking. There were more and more Negro families settling into the neighborhood, Jim noticed. But despite the signs of poverty and neglect that were everywhere, there was also a sense of community here wherever he looked—neighbors conversing from windows across narrow alleys, sharing news, looking out for one another.

He slipped into the front of his building and made his way down a damp hallway to his apartment, his thoughts churning with curiosity and worry about Georgia. A police officer had visited him here at his apartment early this morning to tell him that while a charge had not been formally filed against him for aggravated assault, a personal message from Detective Sam Bohannon had revealed that his leniency would not extend to another incident.

Jim felt a flair of anger at the message. Sam used to be a friend. Hell, he'd recommended Jim's services to Georgia last year. It was how they'd met. Was it Jim's fault that Sam couldn't get over Georgia's peculiarities but didn't want anyone else to have her either?

Life doesn't work like that.

He was well aware that his jealousy of Sam—and there was no other word for it—was because he knew Georgia still wanted him. He ran a hand over his face as if he could physically erase the feelings churning in his gut when he thought of her. She had been right about that. If he couldn't get over it, he needed to fake it better.

The lighting inside his apartment was only what came by a single, dim bulb dangling from a frayed wire in the center of the ceiling. His only furniture besides the single bed in the corner was the phonograph he'd bought when he was discharged from the Army. Its horn was dulled with dust since the machine had sat silent for weeks now. Jim's jazz and ragtime records sat untouched beside the bed. A stack of newspapers, yellowed and curling at the edges, were piled up beside an ashtray overflowing with cigarette butts.

Jim stood for a moment looking at the single room and wondered what Georgia would think if she could see it. He wondered what the stark presentation of his home said about him. In a way, he saw it as a faded echo of who he used to be. Tidy, orderly. Spare. But it had gone past that. The lack of furnishings, the absence of anything homey or warm was nearly pathological.

He went to his bed and sat down, tossing his hat on the floor.. He snaked a cigarette out of the pack on the bedside table and lit up. His eye landed on the photograph he'd taken from Georgia. It too was on his bedside table. Her image was the last thing he saw at night and the first thing he saw in the morning. He picked up the photograph and gazed at her. She was kneeling, her hair tumbling around her shoulders. She was wearing something that looked very like a bathing costume. His eye traced the curve of her body, so easily discernible in the bizarre outfit.

Just before he put it down again, he saw something else that he hadn't seen before. He stood up with the photograph and took it to the single window in his apartment and tilted the photograph to get a better look.

Georgia was on her knees by the bar, the legs of several patrons were near her, but the photograph hadn't captured their faces. But beyond Georgia was a clutch of tables with people sitting at them. Most were out of focus or too far away to make out. All except one. And that one, when Jim looked closely, was a woman wearing a hat pulled low across her face. But not low enough. Jim recognized her immediately.

Janice Gruntz.

The next morning Jim was sitting in his car on the street outside Janice Gruntz's apartment building. Finding Janice in the photograph was the lead they'd been looking for. It meant she'd lied about her whereabouts that night. She had been there the night her sister was killed. Jim had debated half the night about knocking on Janice's door and confronting her with the photograph but eventually decided that was only a viable option if Georgia had come with him. But as it was just him, there was a good chance that approaching Janice alone would send her running terrified for the proverbial hills.

Janice Gruntz's middle-class neighborhood was much nicer than his, although not as nice as Georgia's or Mary's. The streets were clean and some of the houses even featured front yards with trimmed hedges and the occasional flower bed. Jim had gotten here early to explore the area and examine the tidy row of houses that lined the street. He had parked on the street across from Janice Gruntz's building which gave him a clear view of her front door while providing him with sufficient cover. And then he waited, checking his watch from time to time, his foot tapping a silent rhythm, his eyes never straying from the apartment building.

After what felt like a small eternity, the building door finally opened and Janice Gruntz stepped out. She looked both ways down the street, suggesting to Jim that she'd be gone for a while. She was dressed smartly, likely for her daily visit with her mother, although it was a little early for that. Perhaps she had errands first. In any case she didn't linger. Jim waited until she disappeared from view before making his move.

He got out of the car and crossed the street with a casualness that belied his racing heart. He checked over his shoulder to ensure no prying eyes were on him, then slipped around to the back of the building where he was less likely to be seen. He found a back door to each of the individual apartments and quickly identified Janice's. Then, with a set of lock picks —a testament to his preparation—he went to work. Within seconds, the lock gave way with a satisfying click. Jim paused, listening for any sign of unexpected company. Then he opened the door and stepped inside, closing the door quietly behind him.

The interior of Janice's home seemed to be a reflection of suburban normalcy: clean, organized, and simply decorated. Family photos and knick-knacks lined bookshelves in the sitting room where the furniture was in good condition. Jim couldn't help but note that there was a feeling of warmth that his own apartment lacked.

He moved with purpose but also caution, wary of leaving any trace of his presence. He began his search in the living room, sifting through papers, opening drawers. His eyes were constantly scanning for anything out of place, any scrap of evidence that could tie Janice to the crime Georgia was accused of. He noticed that Celeste Latour didn't appear in any of the framed family photos displayed on the bookshelves.

The more he searched, with every passing minute he felt more pressure to find something. He had to believe that every drawer he opened and every cabinet he searched would bring him closer to the truth. The silence in the apartment was a stark backdrop to the loud thumping of his heartbeat. He worked quickly, efficiently, with a growing sense of desperation. He needed to find *something*. He checked the kitchen and then went into the bedroom.

This was the most personally invasive part of the search, he thought with distaste as he went to the bedside lamp table and opened its drawer. Inside was a leather notebook. A diary. He quickly flipped through it. He wouldn't take it if he didn't have to. His eyes scanned the pages, written in a tight, angry handwriting. Within moments, his heart was pounding with excitement. He sat down heavily on the bed and re-read the words in the diary with growing astonishment and excitement.

"I'll kill her with my bare hands. That would be the most satisfying. I need to be careful not to leave any clues for the police —as stupid as they are.

But in a way, I'm not sure getting caught even matters.

Nothing matters except the look on my sister's face when she knows she's about to die."

32

I don't know how I got back to 1924, nor did I care.

I didn't care if all my hair fell out and I woke up on a scaffold with a noose around my neck, or in medieval France about to be burned at the stake. As it was, I landed without incident in the garden behind my townhouse.

I sat in the grass for a moment to let the world stop whirling around me. I reminded myself that in 1924, my mother was yet to be born. She would come back to me in a way even if we never knew each other as mother and daughter. Thinking that helped a little.

I got to my feet and looked toward the house. It was dark and uninviting. I'd left Libby with Mary so there was no one to greet me. But I didn't deserve a greeting or a warm smile. I deserved a cold townhouse and an empty bed. I made my way into the house and up the stairs where I fell into bed fully clothed and slept the rest of the night and most of the next day. I expected my dreams to be full of tragedy and sadness, but I didn't dream at all. That was another blessing I didn't deserve.

When I awoke, it was early afternoon. I lay in bed and heard noises coming from downstairs. Within seconds I heard Libby racing up the stairs before she launched herself onto the bed. I couldn't help reaching out for her and she snuggled into my arms. I buried my head in her fur and held her, my shoulders shaking with the effort not to cry.

"Georgia?" Mary called.

I took in a breath and tried to answer but nothing came out. In a moment, she was standing in my doorway, a look of fear on her face.

"What's happened?" she asked, moving toward the bed.

"Oh, Mary," I said, before bursting into tears.

Instantly she was beside me, her arms around me. I wept into her shoulder, and she patted my back and soothed me while I told her. Then she lay down next to me and just let me cry.

∽

Days later, I sat at my dining room table in front of the French doors. I gazed unseeing through the glass panes of the doors at the garden. My mother loved her own little garden. Especially the roses. My eyes stung and blurred as I looked at the roses in my garden—planted by whoever had owned the townhouse before me—and I wished like I'd never wished for anything before that my mother could see them.

It had been three days since Mary discovered me bereft and heartbroken in my bed. In that time, she'd practically lived with me and every day she had Seamus bring me my meals. I touched the thermos and wrapped egg sandwich that he'd brought a few hours earlier. I thought of the attention that Cook must have put into creating the meals for me at Mary's request.

I knew I needed to hire people to do all this for me if for no other reason than to give Mary's servants a break. She couldn't keep sharing her staff with me. And I know those two. I'm surprised I couldn't hear their grumbling from down the street. On the other hand, I wouldn't be living here much longer. After Sam takes me into custody for the arraignment, I'll wait out the duration of my trial in a jail cell before swapping it for the one on death row. I swallowed hard. No sense in hiring staff.

Libby gave a sharp bark and I turned away from the garden view. Her ears were keener than mine, of course. Sure enough, seconds later, there was a knock at the front door. Libby went tearing to the door, barking loudly. I sat unmoving for a moment. I was pretty sure it was Jim. He'd come by a few other times in the past few days although I hadn't answered the door—or the phone for that matter. I know Mary had spoken to him, so he knew what was going on.

I took in a breath and got to my feet. I was never going to be well. I was never going to be happy. I was never going to forgive myself. But it was probably time to rejoin the living.

"Thought you could use some company," he said, after greeting Libby. His warm eyes probing mine as if to discern how I was, truly.

I realized as soon as I saw him that I was glad he was here. And that surprised me. I think my face must have shown that because his own expression lightened up after he stepped inside. I knew from experience with him that sometimes even just being with him with neither of us talking tended to soothe my nerves. Funny, I'd never realized that before.

I led him into the salon, but he pointed toward the back garden.

"Why don't we get some fresh air?" he suggested. "Has Libby been out today?"

I frowned and looked at Libby. Naturally I hadn't walked her. I let her out when she needed to go. But she preferred to be by my side, not frolicking in the park racing after squirrels.

Jim opened the French doors and Libby immediately dashed outside and down the narrow gravel path weaving in around the azaleas and hydrangea. He tossed a ball to her that I hadn't seen he had in his hand. I stepped out onto the back steps and sat down.

As Libby brought the ball back to drop at his feet, she yipped at him and I laughed in spite of myself. Jim ruffled the dog's fur before launching the ball across the yard again. Libby took off like a bullet, tongue lolling. I watched the two of them do this several times and felt a small knot start to unkink in my chest. It felt good to be outside watching something besides my own thoughts doing battle for my soul. Watching these two play released something tight in my heart. I let out a long sigh.

Stepping back from my grief—even briefly—helped me to see new growth pushing up all around me—in the flowers, in me, and maybe even in the deepening friendship between me and Jim too. For now, in this moment of warmth and companionship, it felt easier to breathe.

After a while, Jim turned and came to sit next to me on the steps. He surprised me by taking my hand before he spoke.

"Mary told me you don't care about proving yourself innocent anymore," he said.

I tried to pull my hand away, but he held it firmly.

"I know you're blaming yourself for your mother's death," he said. "And I reckon it'll take time for you to sort that out."

"I'll never sort it out," I said.

"Okay. I know that focusing on this investigation into who killed Celeste Latour can't replace what you lost. But you should know—we got a lead. Might be nothing, but it's a thread to pull at."

In spite of myself, I felt a stirring in my chest at the prospect of purpose, of moving forward however much I knew I didn't deserve to feel hopeful.

"If you're not ready, that's okay," he said. "I'm going to go on with it until you are."

"You can't do it without me," I said before I knew I was saying it.

He grinned and let go of my hand.

"Alright, then," he said.

"What is it?"

He turned on the step and pulled out a small leather notebook.

"It's Janice Gruntz's diary."

"How did you get it?" I asked as I took it from him and flipped it open.

"I'll tell you that in a minute. But in it, she talks about planning to kill her sister."

I felt a spike of excitement at his words. If true, this was the first real break we'd had in this case since we started investigating. I ran my hand over the cover of the diary and then looked up at the garden again. All of a sudden, I felt my mother near me. I felt her smiling, encouraging me. Tears sprang to my eyes.

"I reckon," Jim said gently, "that your mother wouldn't want you to blame yourself forever."

I nodded. I knew he was right. It just felt perversely good to blame myself. It was something I could do, be angry at myself. Without that, I was left with grief and desolation. I ran my fingers over the indention on the cover that spelled out the words *My Diary*.

"You can't bring her back," Jim said. "But you can clear yourself of this crime. And you know that's what she would want."

I nodded mutely.

"What she writes in there is not exactly a confession," he said. "Especially since Celeste wasn't strangled as it's described in the diary. But it shows the depths of Janice's hatred for her sister and the lengths she would go to get rid of her."

"We need to talk to her again," I said, feeling a flicker of interest rekindle like a warm ember deep in my gut.

"My thoughts exactly," Jim said with a grin. "Preferably without revealing that I committed burglary in the process."

33

The next morning, we decided to catch Janice at Magnolia Manors visiting her mother instead of at her apartment. Presenting her with the diary—while standing in the room where Jim had stolen it—seemed a likely opportunity for Janice to become conveniently distracted from facing the truth. Unfortunately, by the time Jim and I got to Magnolia Manors, the nursing staff remarked that we had just missed her. That was disappointing, but since we were there, we decided to pop in and visit her mother. At first Jim wasn't sure about the point, but as soon as I told him I needed him to keep the old lady occupied, he knew what I was up to.

"Hello, Mrs. Gruntz," Jim said as we walked into her room. "How are you today?"

The old woman looked up at us through cloudy cataracts and frowned. However, I don't care how old you are, when a handsome man pays you attention, it's hard not to respond.

"I've been better," she said, her eyes watching Jim as he pulled up a chair next to her. "I've missed your visits, Alvin."

I glanced at Jim and signaled to him that he should just go with it, but I needn't have bothered. He knew what to do.

"Sorry about that, love," Jim said with an infectious grin as he whipped out the small vase of flowers he'd swiped from the nursing station in the hallway. "Will this help?"

Mrs. Gruntz's eyes lit up at the sight of the flowers and I eased myself out of her line of vision while the two began to talk. First stop for me was to search the bathroom, the most likely place for medicines. I slipped into the bathroom and looked around. The sink, tub and toilet all showed years of use in chipped white porcelain. A row of worn glass bottles sat on the back of the sink. I leaned in to read the labels. They were various tonics for arthritis, headaches and digestion all lined up, some with their apothecary labels still intact. A china cup with painted flowers on it held a single well-worn toothbrush.

On the back of the door a faded bathrobe and nightgown were hung and, on the corner of the bathtub, a bar of lye soap sat in a mesh holder.

I stepped back into the room where Mrs. Gruntz was busy showing Jim something in this month's *Lady's Home Journal*. Just watching him nod his head with occasional *uh huh* kind of loosened something in my diaphragm. I'm not sure what but I don't think many men could've played this role quite as well.

I moved to the bed and the nightstand. There was a worn Bible along with yet another pill bottle on top of the nightstand. And a small amber glass medicine bottle. With a quick glance over my shoulder at the two in the sitting room area, I picked up the bottle and read the label: *Digoxin*.

I took out my phone and snapped a photo of the bottle propped next to the newspaper that I'd bought that morning showing today's date before we came. I knew of course that I couldn't set this photo in front of Sam as proof —nor did I know how to get my digital photographs printed in 1924—but I felt better with visual evidence of what I'd found.

I motioned to Jim to wrap things up and he immediately stood up. I once more made myself visible to Mrs. Gruntz who instantly huffed.

"Did you clean under the bed?" she asked me.

"Yes, ma'am," I said.

I edged out of the room with Jim right behind me.

"You're not going to believe what I found," I said.

"Was it medicine for her heart condition?" he asked with a smile.

On the drive back into town we were both nearly throbbing with excitement. Now we had motive, means and opportunity for Janice. All I had to do now was present it to Sam. The more I thought of that, the less I liked the idea. Sam had already shown himself to be resistant to any of my ideas about the case. The fact was, I needed a confession.

Once we got to town, we went straight to the Cottonmouth Club. I thought about going to Janice's apartment for a showdown with her but decided I needed to dot a few more i's before then. I didn't want to present my case to Sam and have him poke holes in it. I needed to do my due diligence. And that meant talking to the other so-called suspects to rule them out. I wanted to go to the Cottonmouth Club because, for me, everything about this case centered around the speakeasy. First, of course, because the victim was killed there, but also because it seemed that her killer had a special connection to the place. I'm not sure why I felt that way and I have no concrete evidence to support the theory. But I put a lot of stock in intuition.

Which was why it was so jarring when we turned the corner into the alley that led to the entrance of the club and saw a sign plastered over the side door that read CLOSED BY ORDER OF THE POLICE.

I felt a wave of confusion. It was beyond belief that the place had been raided by the police *and* someone murdered there, yet it had stayed open for business then but was now mysteriously closed.

"Now what?" I asked, flustered.

"Now we bell a few cats in their lairs," Jim said with a shrug.

It was threatening rain by the time Jim and I arrived at the Marshall House Hotel on Broughton Street. Neither of us had forgotten that Don Berford had reported our last run-in with him to the police—which I still thought was outrageous, considering he'd thrown the first punch. I imagine it was a classic case of rich Hollywood tycoon not believing the rules applied to him.

After entering the hotel lobby, Jim and I decided to try and catch Berford on his way out rather than confront him in his hotel room. After the last fracas, a public venue seemed more prudent than a private confrontation where the little weasel could accuse us of assaulting him. We lingered in the lobby, pretending to peruse brochures at the reception desk as we kept an eye on the elevator.

When the elevator finally announced its arrival at the lobby level with a chime, Don Berford emerged and we made our move. We casually fell in step behind him, following him through the lobby toward the front door. Just before he reached the entrance, Don paused to pat his pockets for cigarettes. When he did, I reached out and touched his arm.

"Excuse me, Mr. Berford," I said.

Berford turned and glanced at both me and Jim.

"Not you two again," he growled.

"We'll just take a moment of your time," Jim said as he effectively blocked the man's only exit.

Berford glanced at the registration desk and then around the lobby. I'm not sure whether he was hoping for reinforcements or witnesses.

"We're happy to follow you out into the street," I said. "We can talk as we walk."

Berford's posture stiffened once he realized there was no escaping us. He folded his arms tightly across his chest, a defensive gesture that revealed just how unhappy he was to see us.

"Fine," he grumbled, "Ask your questions."

"Where were you the night your wife was killed?" Jim asked.

"How dare you!?"

"Oh, stop posturing!" I said irritably. "Do you have an alibi or not?"

"I did not kill my wife! I loved my wife!"

"Said every wife killer ever," I said. "So what's your alibi?"

"I was with my wife that night as usual," he said between gritted teeth.

"So, no alibi," I said.

He turned on me, his temper once more showing itself, but he hesitated and glanced at Jim before bringing himself under control.

"Fine," he said. "I don't have an alibi *per se*. But the police don't think that's a problem."

"Why don't they?" asked Jim. "Is it because they can see how devastated you are about your wife's sudden demise?"

Berford went red in the face and clenched his hands into fists. I could see he wanted to turn on Jim with the how-dare-you approach he'd tried on me, but he must have seen by the expressions on our faces that it would be a waste of time.

"I won't honor that with an answer," he said.

"Okay," I said. "Let's take a different tact. You were overheard saying you wanted to be free of your wife."

"That's a lie!"

"*I* was the one who overheard it," I said. "So, I'm not inclined to think it is a lie."

He visibly whitened.

"Then you...you misunderstood."

"Great. Let's clear it up. What did you mean by saying you wanted to be free?"

"I'm sure I didn't say *I* wanted to be free. I wanted *Celeste* to be free of the script she'd just signed onto. You can ask Tomlinson. I assume that's the conversation you're referring to?"

This surprised and unsettled me for a moment. Clearly, Berford remembered the conversation I was referring to and, now that I think about it, his words *could've* been referencing a contract that was not marital. Had I jumped the gun thinking it was a prenup he was trying to get out of?

"What was wrong with the script?" I asked, trying to buy some time while I thought where I was going with him now.

"For starters, she would be playing the mother in the movie," he said. "Naturally, Celeste wasn't thrilled with that."

That actually jived with what Murphy had said.

"Plus, the money wasn't what we were expecting," he said.

I saw Jim glance at me, silently asking me if I had

anything else I wanted to ask him. But since Berford had annoyingly come up with a plausible explanation for what I thought was a seriously indicting conversation, I had nothing.

"Is that it?" Berford asked, clearly picking up that Jim and I had lost steam on questioning him. "Besides, the cops told me that Celeste was poisoned with heart medicine."

"What difference does the type of poison make?" Jim asked.

"Well, I would've thought the cops would be more interested in finding where Celeste's personal assistant was during the time in question," Berford said.

My heart began to speed up.

"Millie Ross?" I asked. "Why?"

"Because everybody knows Millie is the one with the bad heart."

34

"How did we not know this?" I asked Jim an hour later in a booth at the diner on Bull Street.

"I guess we weren't asking the right questions," he said as he salted his meatloaf and mashed potatoes and signaled to the waitress for more coffee.

"So much for thinking Millie and Berford might have been having an affair," I said.

Jim frowned. "Were you thinking that?"

"It crossed my mind. But now I know they weren't. I mean he threw her under the bus."

"The expressions you come up with," he said shaking his head.

Jennie came over and poured his coffee while snapping her gum. Her eyes were bright as she smiled at him.

"Thank you," Jim said.

"Any time, sugar," she said as she sashayed away.

I looked at my own empty coffee cup. Oh well. I hadn't really made too many deep friendships from my brief stint here as a waitress.

"So, Millie Ross should be staying at the Marshall House too, same as Tomlinson and Don Berford, right?" I asked.

"Unless she left to go back to California," he said.

"I wonder," I said. "Do you remember Tomlinson saying Millie didn't have lots of money? Would the studio pay for her to return? Or is she unemployed now?"

"Those are all good questions, and we should definitely ask her when we find her," he said, pouring sugar into his coffee.

There was something different about Jim today and I couldn't put my finger on what it was. In a way, I had gone away and got blindsided with the most devastating news that a person can get with my mother dying. And Jim didn't miss a beat but just stepped in to be the friend I really and truly needed.

"Do I have mustard on my chin?" he asked, rubbing his face with a napkin.

I laughed.

"No, sorry. I didn't mean to stare."

∼

After that, we spent an hour hanging around the lobby of the Marshall House until eventually losing patience and going upstairs to knock on Millie's room door but there was no answer. We toyed with the idea of splitting up with one of us staking out the hotel while the other went in search of Janice who was still our main suspect and someone with whom we really needed to have a major sit down. But in the end, I don't think either of us wanted to go off without the other. I know Jim was thinking he needed to stay near me because I was still so emotionally vulnerable—or whatever the words for that were in 1924. And he wasn't wrong.

Right now, for whatever reason, I appreciated his company. So, when we gave up on talking to Millie for the moment at the hotel, we headed over to where Janice Gruntz lived to see what she had to say about the evidence we'd uncovered that pointed directly at her for her sister's murder.

The building where Janice Gruntz lived was not located in a ghetto, but neither was it terribly nice and could only loosely be defined as middle class. I could almost imagine the resentment she must have felt seeing from all the fan magazines how her sister lived in Beverly Hills.

"Janice was definitely not enjoying any of Celeste's wealth," I commented as we made our way into the run-down building.

I paused at her door and listened with my ear to it for a moment but didn't hear anything except the sounds of a phonograph record playing some soft jazz. I knocked and within seconds the music stopped. A moment after that, Janice opened the door and looked at us in surprise.

"What do you want?" she asked, only opening the door a crack.

"Just a few minutes of your time, Miss Gruntz," Jim said.

"I'm sorry," she said. "Now is not a good time for visitors."

As she tried to shut the door Jim stuck his foot in the opening. Her eyes widened in fear and outrage.

"Move your foot! How dare you?!"

Instead, Jim pushed open the door and we stepped into the apartment.

"How dare you!" she shrieked. "I will call the police!"

She ran to the phone and picked up the receiver and turned and glared at us but there was more fear than outrage in her expression.

"By all means, call them," I said as I pulled out her diary. "I'm just going to read from this interesting book we found while we wait for them—at which point, I think they'll be interested in reading it, too."

I opened the book and found a passage.

"*I'll kill her with my bare hands. That will be the most satisfying. But I need to be careful not to leave any clues for the police—*"

"How dare you!?" Janice shrieked as she snatched the book from my hands.

She ran to a window in the small living room that faced a back alley, the book clutched to her chest.

"I'll have you arrested for theft!" she said, trembling violently as she faced us.

"We didn't steal it," I said. "We found it in the street. Actually, we're good Samaritans by returning it to you."

"I never take it out of this room so that's a lie," Janice said, her chest heaving with emotion.

"Well, good luck proving it," I said with a shrug. "And in the meantime, that excerpt I just read about killing your sister with your bare hands will be Exhibit A in the prosecution's case against you at your murder trial."

"Murder...?"

She looked from me to Jim and back again, the expression on her face one of mounting horror.

"Surely, you must see how this looks," I said reasonably. "And how it will look to a jury."

"Stop it! Stop it this instance! I did not kill my sister!"

"Where were you on the night of April fifth?" Jim asked.

She looked at him, her face flushed.

"I was nowhere near where the murder took place!"

I made a loud buzzer sound.

"Wrong answer," I said as I pulled out the photograph

Sam had given me. "If I may direct the jury's attention to the defendant pictured here in this photograph taken the night of the murder."

I pointed to the image of Janice sitting not two seats away from Celeste. Janice immediately began to nervously twist the rings on her fingers.

"I can explain," she said, her eyes on the photograph as if it might jump up and bite her.

"And we can't wait to hear it," I said. "Mind if we sit?"

Janice watched us sit in the chairs in her living room. She seemed stunned that she couldn't stop this from happening.

"By the way," I said, "you don't have to worry about losing that diary again." I pointed to how she was clinging to it. "I can see it's important to you. So we made a copy."

With a whimper, she sat down on the couch, her shoulders sagging in defeat.

"It's not what you think," she said.

"Enlighten us," I said.

She shook her head and a rough laugh came out of her, surprising me.

"I'm writing a book," she said. "A book about growing up with the famous Celeste Latour, nee Cece Gruntz."

"Good job changing her name," I commented.

Janice responded to my interruption with a scowl.

"I'm writing a book as a catharsis," she said. "My psychiatrist said it would be...healing for me."

I wondered briefly if doctors had the same HIPAA-style limitations as they did in my time. One way or the other, someone needed to take a deposition with this psychiatrist.

"Prove you're writing a book," I said.

She hesitated only a moment and then stood up and went to her desk. She put the diary in a drawer and locked it and then went to another drawer and pulled out a thin stack of typewriter pages. She came back to us and with shaking hands handed the stack to me.

On the top of the first page was written: *My Life with My Monster Celebrity Sister*.

I flipped through a few pages and then handed the stack to Jim. On the face of it, it was entirely possible that the diary was only source material for this memoir and not a plan of action at all. And if the psychiatrist did allow the police to look at his case notes on Janice where he had suggested this kind of writing project as a therapeutic exercise, then I was pretty sure we were looking at crossing Janice Gruntz off our suspects list.

Jim must have thought the same thing because he handed the sheets back to Janice with a disappointed sigh.

"What about the photograph?" I asked. "You were at the club that night."

She sighed shakily. "I was."

"Why?"

"It was stupid. I wanted to talk to my sister."

"Wouldn't it have been easier to just pick up the phone?"

She laughed again and shook her head in disgust.

"She wasn't taking my calls."

The rest of our conversation with Janice revealed little more. There was a perfectly reasonable explanation for every piece of evidence we thought we had against her. While it was true that the threats in the diary were shocking, in the end they were just words, not in themselves a vow of intention. The angry statements she'd written didn't mean she *didn't* make good on her threats. But just by themselves, they weren't enough.

As Jim and I were letting ourselves out of her apartment —both of us once more battling disappointment—I stiffened my resolve and reminded myself that the diary nonetheless did still point to motive. And the photograph proved Janice had opportunity. Filling out this little trifecta with means was the memory of Janice's mother's bedside table and what would have been incredibly easy access to the poison that all experts agreed had killed her sister.

35

After leaving Janice's apartment, even after telling myself that she only had her word to refute the evidence we'd laid before her—and that she still ticked all the boxes for motive, opportunity and means—I still felt an overwhelming discouragement about our interview with her. It occurred to me that it was possible that what I was feeling was simple exhaustion. Sometimes time traveling takes it out of me physically beyond the aging-before-my-time thing. It wrings me out on just about every level. I was glad Jim wasn't in a talkative mood after we left Janice's. All I could think of was that I wanted to go home and crawl into bed.

After he drove me home, he offered to walk Libby for me and even to make dinner, but I just wanted to be alone. I think he understood. I didn't get the sense that he was sulking. He probably could see the exhaustion written across my face and in every movement of my body.

That night, in fact, I skipped Libby's walk altogether, and just let her out into the back garden to do her business. I scrounged up dinner with whatever I could find in the pantry which turned out to be more Ramen noodles which I ate with a Diet Coke. Because the twenties weren't very advanced when it came to dog food, I'd brought back several bags of individual wet dog food packets. I figured I was at least a hundred years away from having to worry about single use containers filling up the landfills. Besides, I'm not sure there *were* even any landfills at this point.

In any case, I showered and got ready for bed before it was even dark and was fast asleep before my head hit the pillow.

The next morning, Jim was busy with his own clients again, so I allowed myself some time to putter around the townhouse and do a few things like watering the garden and washing dishes that had piled up, until our planned get together in the afternoon. We were going back to the hotel to try to talk to Millie.

I was in the process of sorting the laundry when the phone rang. I assumed it was either Jim or Mary since nobody else called me, so I was surprised to hear an unfamiliar woman's voice on the line.

"Miss Belle? This is Ruby James. From the diner?"

"Yes, Ruby," I said. "I remember you."

"I got your number from Mr. Johnson from when you worked here because I heard something I thought you should know."

There were background sounds of a kitchen on her end and I wondered if she was using the diner's office phone to call me.

"I heard about you being arrested for that movie star's murder," she said, "and I thought how nice you were to me and if I could help I would."

"That's very nice of you, Ruby," I said. "Thank you."

"So, when I saw the assistant to that movie star come in

here a few minutes ago for lunch, I thought maybe you'd want to know."

I was on my feet before she finished speaking.

Millie is at the diner?

"She's there now?" I asked, my voice betraying my excitement.

"Yes, ma'am, she surely is. And since I seen her fight with that movie star more than once, I thought maybe she had something to hide about how she died."

"I cannot thank you enough, Ruby," I said, already grabbing my hat and looking around for my purse.

"Don't thank me, Miss Belle," Ruby said. "Kindness ain't easy to find in this town."

Thanking her profusely anyway, I hung up, grabbed my jacket and found my purse on the table in the foyer and ran out the door.

~

I find it so startling to walk into a restaurant—even a small-town diner like this one on Bull Street—and see all the swirling smoke above the booths. It hadn't even been in my lifetime that people used to smoke in restaurants. Or if it had, I was too young to remember.

I spotted Millie from the doorway and signaled to Jennie the waitress that I would be joining her booth. Country tunes twanged from the radio behind the counter as I walked down the aisle where Millie sat, a newspaper spread before her. A half-empty plate of cottage cheese and peaches sat on the table beside a cup of coffee.

"My, my," I said as I sat down across from her, causing her to look up in unhappy surprise. "Are we on a diet?

Because take it from me, the pot roast and fried potatoes here are to die for."

"What do you want?" Millie asked as she surreptitiously scraped some coins she'd been counting out on the table into her palm.

It was obvious she was counting pennies to see how much she could afford to eat. I don't care how much you're watching your calories. Peaches and cottage cheese is downright draconian. I signaled the waitress and Jennie came over.

"Hey, Georgia," she said. "What'll you have?"

"I won't be able to resist the pot roast, Jennie," I said. "Can I have it with a pot of coffee and a big slice—no, make that two big slices—of Charlie's apple pie?"

"With ice cream?"

"How else?"

I turned back to Millie as she watched me with one hand curled tightly around her empty coffee cup.

"So, I understand you have a heart condition," I said.

She blanched. "Who told you that?"

"Is it not true?"

She gulped and looked down at the table.

"No, it's true."

"Do the police know?"

She looked up at me in a flash.

"I didn't kill her."

"Even if that's true," I said patiently, "the fact that you had the drug that killed her is incriminating. Were your drugs locked up in a safe?"

She made a face.

"What? Why would they be? They're not valuable."

Just then Jennie showed up with a tray of food with which she covered the table. I watched Millie eye the food hungrily. I poured myself a cup of coffee and pulled one of the slices of pie over toward me.

"My point is," I said, picking up a fork, "if your heart pills were easy to access—"

A look of comprehension fluttered across her face.

"I carry them in my purse," she said.

Just as I feared. It meant that anyone could've had access to them. It didn't take Millie off the hot seat—far from it—but it also made it possible for just about anybody at the Cottonmouth Club that night to use them to kill Celeste.

Millie's stomach let out an audible growl.

"Please help yourself," I said, biting into the apple pie as the ice cream dripped down the sides. "I already had lunch and I guess my eyes were bigger than my stomach."

Millie picked up her fork and then put it down. I had to hand it to her. I don't know how long she'd been skipping meals to save money but if she'd been dependent on Celeste for pocket money, she was probably pretty hungry by now.

"Eat, Millie," I said. "You don't benefit anyone by starving yourself."

She hesitated only a moment before she pulled the plate of pot roast and potatoes to her and began to eat. I steeled myself from being moved at the sight. Just because she was suffering didn't mean she didn't kill Celeste. And even if she had good reason for killing her, murder was still wrong.

Not to mention the fact that I was being held accountable for the crime.

"You and Celeste didn't get along, did you?" I asked.

She paused a moment in her eating and then took a long sip from the coffee I'd just poured in her cup.

"People heard you arguing," I said. "There were witnesses."

"Celeste was a monster," Millie said, finally pushing

away from the pot roast. "She lived to make my life miserable."

Now I don't know a lot about being an assistant to a movie star, but I imagine as bosses, those kinds of people can be pretty onerous. If you have any sense of self-worth, it might be hard to endure their criticism and constant demands.

Unless there was something more?

"You hated her," I suggested and then waited.

She looked at me and her eyes filled with tears. I wondered if she could do that on command. If so, *now* was a perfect time to do it.

"I did," she whispered. "I hated her."

"It wasn't just that she was unreasonable?" I prompted. "There was something else?"

She nodded and looked down at her hands. "There was," she said.

"Can you tell me?"

She shook her head.

"If I did, you'd never believe I didn't kill her."

36

"I can't believe you met with her without me," Jim said a few hours later when he phoned me at the townhouse.

I'd come home long enough to feed and walk Libby and grab a bite to eat. When he called, I had just put away my laptop where I'd been making notes on the case.

"I don't think she would've talked as freely if you'd been there," I said.

"That's fair," he said. "But I hope you were careful that she didn't put anything in your drink."

"Haha. Funny guy. But seriously, if I had to give an opinion of whether or not Millie looked like she hated Celeste Latour enough to kill her, I'd have to say, honestly, that she did. But having said that, I really didn't get murderous vibes off her."

"Sometimes I don't understand your words."

"I didn't get the feeling that Millie killed her boss."

"You can't trust your feelings too much," he said. "What about Janice? How does your gut think about her?"

"She just doesn't feel right to me either."

"I have to say I tend to agree. But we can't discount either of them. Gut or no, they're still suspects."

"Absolutely. Plus, we haven't finished questioning Berford. He admitted he has no alibi."

"True. And he definitely seems just the type to poison his wife. It's sneakier than strangling."

"I agree."

"What about Tomlinson?"

"We have nothing on him," I reminded him.

"Isn't that what you'd expect from a slick agent?"

"What are you suggesting?" I asked.

"I'm not sure how much good a *conversation* with a weasel will do," he said.

"I'm listening."

"We need to search his hotel room."

∼

The sun hung low in the sky, casting an orange glow over the street in front of the Marshal House as Jim and I waited on a park bench across the street to see if Tomlinson would leave. A sultry warmth seemed to cling in the thick air, but I felt an undeniable edge of electricity that promised an oncoming storm.

We sat obscured from view from the hotel by a clutch of azalea bushes, its flowers mostly spent. Evening traffic was sparse, consisting mostly of a couple horse and buggies and pedestrians hurrying home before the weather broke. It was already nearly dark, but the hotel was lighted up sufficient to give us a good view. Through the hotel windows, shadows passed back and forth like marionettes on a stage, oblivious to the fact that eyes were watching from the outside.

I have to say I thought what we were doing—although

slightly terrifying—was basically a good idea. There are some people who lie as easily as breathing, and they are usually the ones who are notoriously difficult to determine if they are lying. I didn't relish the idea of spending an hour with Tomlinson while he gathered all kinds of Intel on what we knew and more importantly what we didn't, while Jim and I walked away none the wiser. I also didn't love the idea of breaking and entering—especially since getting caught would be catastrophic for both of us—but I just didn't see another avenue to help us get what we needed. And honestly, after Jim's positive results going through Janice Gruntz's apartment, I was ready to give home invasion a real shot.

Minute by minute, gloaming deepened into darkness like a veil drawn across the sky. Streetlamps flickered on one by one, golden flecks punctuating the night. I sat rigidly on the bench while Jim leaned nonchalantly into it. Both of us kept our eyes on the hotel's entrance, waiting for the moment when Tomlinson would emerge. It wasn't likely he'd spend an evening alone in his hotel room. Even if the Cottonmouth Club was closed. There were other speakeasies in town. We were counting on that anyway.

As the first droplets fell and faint rumbles heralded the impending storm, I began to rock in place as anxiety thrummed through me.

"What's taking him so long?" I said.

"He'll leave. No way he's spending all night in there alone."

"Maybe he's not alone."

"Now that's an interesting thought," Jim said giving me a sidelong look. "Anybody in mind?"

"I'm not sure," I said. "I thought he sounded pretty protective of Millie."

"You noticed that, too, did you?"

Suddenly Tomlinson emerged from the hotel.

"Showtime," I said, standing up.

As soon as we saw Tomlinson pull up his collar and dash down the front steps of the hotel into the waiting taxi that he must have had the concierge call for him, the downpour began in earnest. Jim and I waited until the cab was out of sight before hurrying across the street to slip into the hotel lobby. Most patrons were either dining in town or had retreated to their rooms upstairs, leaving the lobby empty.

We skipped the elevator and walked to the stairwell, our shoes making barely a sound as we went. We'd already gotten the information that Tomlinson's room was on the second floor and went straight to it. We stood outside his door a moment, listening, but all was quiet. Jim pulled out a small packet of tool picks and made quick work of opening the lock. I marveled at how easy it was in this decade. No electronic key cards to fuss with. Once the tumblers fell into place, he turned the doorknob and pushed open the door.

Inside, a single lamp cast the living area in dim light as the rain hammered the windows. Books and papers were scattered on the writing desk next to the bed. Jim headed to the bathroom while I went for the bedside table.

There was a pack of Lucky Strike cigarettes, a very full ashtray, and a couple of hotel book matches on the table next to the bedside lamp as well as a small notebook. I immediately flipped through the notebook. There were a few dates—mostly in the past, and a phone number with the letter *M* next to it. I glanced at the hotel phone prefix on the phone and noted that the phone number prefix in the notebook was the same.

M for Millie?

I left the notebook where I found it and opened the nightstand drawer. Inside were more cigarettes, a small bottle of hair pomade, nail scissors and a pack of gum.

Discouraged, I turned to the desk just as Jim emerged from the bathroom.

"Any joy?" I asked.

He shook his head.

"A razor, a bottle of rye whiskey, toothbrush. You?"

"Not yet. Except it looks as if he and Millie are definitely a thing."

I went to the desk and opened the desk drawer and found hotel note pads and a file folder.

"Here we go," I said with excitement as I pulled the folder out.

Jim came to look over my shoulder as I opened the folder. Inside was a single piece of paper. After a moment of scanning the document, Jim whistled.

"This changes everything," he said.

It certainly did. I was holding a letter drafted by a Los Angeles law firm representing Celeste Latour formally terminating her employment contract with Gerald Tomlinson effective immediately.

The letter was dated the day that Celeste was murdered.

37

"I'd say we just found our smoking gun," Jim said as we both stared at the letter.

Just then, we heard the sound of a key in the room door. We snapped our heads around to look. My adrenaline shot out the roof as I watched the doorknob turn. There was no time to do anything. Not even enough time to hide under the bed or jump out a window. As I prayed it was just the housekeeping team, the door swung open revealing Gerald Tomlinson.

Tomlinson stood in the doorway, staring at us, his eyes blazing with fury.

"What is the meaning of this?!" he roared.

There really wasn't much for Jim or I to say at this point and by the way Tomlinson was blocking our exit, it was clear he too thought the time for action was upon us. Fortunately, Jim outweighed the Hollywood agent by a good thirty pounds, plus his martial arts skills were honed to a tee. Without a word, Jim advanced upon Tomlinson and threw an elbow into the man's face knocking him off balance and into the door jamb. He then shot out a hand

and grabbed my hand, jerking me to the door before turning and pushing Tomlinson, who was already teetering precariously, onto his backside onto the floor.

Then we ran. We ran down the stairwell to the lobby and through it. Jim was ahead of me but not by much. The concierge looked up in concern from his desk as we ran which I knew meant he'd be able to give a description of us to support Tomlinson's charge of breaking and entering. But I didn't have time to think about that now. Once outside, Jim led me to a narrow alley that separated the hotel from the adjacent building. We both took a moment to catch our breath before turning and heading down the alley to the next darkened street.

To say we didn't stop running until we reached Jim's car three blocks away would be an exaggeration, but not by much. My heart was pounding from the exertion and the fact of our discovery as much as by my horror that Tomlinson had caught us in the act. I had every expectation that the police would be waiting on my doorstep for us. We took side streets back to my place and Jim parked a block away. We left his car and hurried toward my townhouse where we found a hiding spot across the street shrouded by azaleas where we could watch my townhouse without being seen. Jim sat propped against a gnarled magnolia tree trunk, while I perched on a rickety moss-draped bench.

"I can't believe that *we're* the ones on the run," I said. "We've got proof now that Tomlinson had a strong motive for murder."

"Yeah, except proof of a motive isn't proof of the murder," Jim said.

"Whatever," I said with annoyance.

I was instantly sorry I snapped at him, especially since I knew my pique was really directed at Sam since he was the one forcing Jim and me into subterfuge—not to mention breaking and entering—in order to get the necessary proof to clear me.

As a tense silence fell between us, the night breeze carried what sounded like spooky whispers through Spanish moss. My gaze drifted across the street to the front of my porch. As my eyes adjusted to darkness, a peripheral movement caught my eye. I turned around to see it was Jim leaning toward me. I leaned toward him, thinking he was going to whisper something to me when his hand cupped my cheek and, turning my face upwards, he leaned down and kissed me.

It was so unexpected that for a split second I did nothing. And then I kissed him back, my pulse quickening. I finally pulled away and searched his face but in the dark, shadows masked his expression. I didn't know what the kiss meant and I was too confused to try to figure it out at the moment. So I turned away and focused on the scene of my own front porch again.

"Maybe he didn't call the police?" I asked softly.

I heard Jim sigh and then move back to where he'd been sitting before he kissed me.

"Why would he not call the police?" he said. "We broke into his room!"

"He might not," I said, "if he thought he had more to lose by talking to them."

I pulled out the termination letter we'd found just before Tomlinson had interrupted us. Jim had had the forethought to quickly stuff it into his jacket pocket. The best way for this letter to get called into evidence at my murder trial and used against Tomlinson was for him to have us arrested tonight. He had to know that the first thing we'd do was show Sam the letter.

"I don't think he reported the break in," I said.

"It is starting to look that way. So now what?"

I still wasn't thrilled at the thought of going home even though there appeared to be no real activity at my house. I took in a shaky breath and turned and handed the letter to Jim.

"Wait for me," I said.

Before he could respond, I stood up and hurried across the dark street to my front door. Within minutes, I'd confirmed that nobody was waiting for us inside—except a very anxious terrier needing to pee.

38

An hour later Jim and I were sitting in Mary's dining room trying to pool together all the evidence and clues we'd found so far in order to figure out who the killer could be.

I pointed to the copy of the letter we'd stolen from Tomlinson's room now laying on Mary's dining room table.

"That's a major motive," I said.

"Agreed," Mary said. "But it doesn't address how Tomlinson got the poison."

"There's a possibility he got the poison from Millie," I said.

Mary's eyes widened.

"Are you suggesting Millie and Tomlinson murdered Celeste together?" she asked.

I glanced at Jim. Ever since the kiss he'd been unusually quiet.

"It's possible," I said. "On the other hand, I saw Millie go to the ladies room the night the club was raided and I noticed she left her handbag at the table."

"Surely that was unusual?" Mary said in near horror.

"I have to admit, I thought it strange," I said.

"Do you think she kept her heart pills in her bag?" Jim asked with a frown.

"I don't know," I said. "But she was traveling so she might have."

"It strikes me that leaving her bag on the table might be a good way to allow someone else to steal the drugs from it," Mary said thoughtfully.

"You think she was looking for an escape clause in case she was accused?" Jim asked.

"It's a thought," Mary said.

"Okay, let's look at this again," I said. "Millie has motive, opportunity and means. Check, check, and check."

"Don Berford has all three too," Mary pointed out.

"As does Patrick Murphy," I said. "Although his motive is pretty shaky."

"Don't forget Gerald Tomlinson," Jim said. "Whether he was working with Millie or alone, he's got all three, too. Motive, opportunity and, thanks to Millie's open purse, means."

"Right," I said, glad to see that Jim was participating in the discussion and not moping over the kiss. "And Janice has all three too since the fact that she was in the photograph proves she was there that night. She had access to her mother's heart medicine. And she hated her sister."

"That's five suspects," Mary said. "Surely, we can find the killer among *five* suspects!"

"But which of the five?" I asked in frustration. "Any one of them *could* be guilty but probably only one is. Probably."

My mind reached back to an old Agatha Christie novel where in fact there was no *one* guilty party—all the suspects had pitched in on the kill. I thought about the possibility that Don Berford, Tomlinson, Janice and Millie were in on this. But then I realized that I had to take Janice out of the equation. Like Murphy, she was an outsider and wouldn't have been a part of any joint murder agreement.

So did the three in Celeste's entourage conspire to kill her? But if so, then why would Berford mention that Millie took blood pressure medicine? That would be a sure way to shine the light on her and, if he was complicit, he couldn't help but come under scrutiny as well. No, the group murder angle didn't hold.

"Georgia?" Mary prompted.

"In my experience," I said, giving Mary a meaningful look so she would know I was talking about my time in the future, "detectives often gather all the suspects together in one room and address each one, laying out all the evidence until one of them breaks."

"Does that usually work?" Jim asked, clearly skeptical.

"Almost every time," I lied.

Honestly, I'd only seen it work in novels and movies, but at the point we were I thought it was worth a try.

"Do they always show up?" Mary asked.

"They do, but we should do something to ensure they do."

"Like what?"

"Like a letter," I said. "We'll deliver a letter to each of them offering them something they want."

"Okay. First question, who are our main suspects?" Mary asked, picking up a pencil as if ready to make a list.

"Millie, Don Berford, Tomlinson and Janice." After a moment, I added Murphy, too.

"Okay. And what do we offer them to get them to come?" Jim asked.

"That's easy," I said. "For Tomlinson it's the letter we took tonight. He might not go to the police, but he definitely wants it back. For Millie, it's money. For Berford, it's a page from Celeste's diary where she claims he's gay and she's on the verge of telling the world."

"He's what?" Mary asked, looking at me in confusion.

"Homosexual."

"Goodness! Is that true?" she asked in surprise.

"I have no idea, but I assume it's a stigma in 1924?"

Immediately, we both glanced nervously at Jim.

"You say the strangest things," he said, shaking his head.

"Yes, of course it's a stigma," Mary said quickly as if trying to cover for my odd statement.

"As for Janice," I said, "we offer another diary section where Celeste says how sorry she was about the way she treated her mother and sister."

"Would that be enough to lure her?" Jim asked.

I tapped a pencil against my lip, thinking.

"Good point. If Janice killed her sister, she did it out of resentment and a desire for revenge, agreed?"

The other two nodded their heads.

"So maybe instead of an apology, we tell Janice that Celeste wrote a letter that she gave to Millie saying that if anything happened to her, the police should look to her sister first."

"Better," Jim said.

"But that only works if she's the killer," Mary pointed out.

"She'll come even if she's not the killer," I said. "If for no other reason than to get her hands on the letter so she doesn't have to defend herself against a false charge sometime in the future."

"And Patrick Murphy?" Mary asked with a frown.

"For Murphy, we just tell the truth," I said. "We send him a note saying we're gathering all the suspects in one group. We'll tell him we no longer consider him a suspect, but we would like him to be there in case he remembers something during the questioning that will help us narrow down who the killer is. I'll phrase the letter as a personal favor to me since I'm the one who's on the hook for going to prison."

Both Jim and Mary agreed that was the best approach with Murphy. As we were discussing it, a thought came to me. A thought out of the blue in many ways but still one worth paying attention, I thought.

"There's just one little thing that will put the proverbial icing on this cake," I said turning to Jim. "Do you think you can get into the employee locker room at the police station tonight without being seen?"

He shrugged.

"I can try. Just tell me what I'm looking for."

∼

A couple hours later after composing all the letters, I waited until Jim left to try his luck at the police station and to deliver the letters before turning to Mary.

"What's happened?" she asked, her eyes full of concern. "Something has happened."

"Jim kissed me."

Her face cleared.

"My, you have had an eventful evening," she said.

"I didn't know how to react when it happened."

"Does that mean you didn't enjoy it?"

"Mary, stop it. I don't want to hurt him."

"So don't."

"I feel so disloyal."

"To whom?" Mary's eyes widened in outrage. "To *Sam*?!"

"I know you don't understand."

"No, I don't. Can I ask you something, Georgia?"

When I didn't answer, she took it as tacit agreement.

"I was just wondering what you think your mother would think of how Sam has treated you," she said.

I felt my heart begin to ache at her words.

"That's not fair," I whispered.

"So much in life isn't," she said, reaching over to squeeze my hand. "But I'll ask you to think about it just the same."

39

It was nearly three in the morning by the time Jim and I arrived at the Cottonmouth Club. He had hand delivered the letters we'd written at Mary's and gotten begrudging assurances from all five suspects that they would meet us at the club. Jim and I left Mary's as soon as he got back so that we'd get to the club before anyone else, but Don Berford was already there waiting. I could see by the look on his face that he was seriously agitated. After what he'd read in the letter we'd handed him, that would be for good reason. A public accusation of sexual deviation—which was what homosexuality was considered in 1924—would be the end of his career in Hollywood.

He didn't bother greeting us, but stood with his arms crossed, glaring and waiting as Jim used his lock-picking tools to open the front door. Inside, the usually bustling and lively Cottonmouth Club was eerily vacant, the only life coming from a few light bulbs flickering overhead.

"I want to see this document you say you have," Berford said angrily, as we entered the club.

"All in good time, Mr. Berford," I said, soothingly

gesturing to a door leading to one of the smaller rooms in the club across from the dance floor.

Normally these smaller rooms were used for clandestine deals or romantic liaisons. Jim and I'd given some thought to where we were going to set up for our mass confrontation. We had decided that the neighborhood beat cop might interrupt us if we turned the lights on in the main area of the club. Inside the smaller room was a large wooden table in the center of the room where we could lay out our proof. The space was perfect for our needs. Jim started arranging a line of chairs.

"Take a seat," he said to Berford before going back out to the front door of the club to greet the other suspects as they arrived.

"What's the hold up?" Berford said as he sat down and cracked his knuckles in agitation.

"We are waiting for a few more people," I said mildly.

Just then, Millie Ross came into the room on the arm of Gerald Tomlinson. Seeing them together, I have to say that Tomlinson looked less like her lover than her caretaker. She seemed very fragile. Haunted, even. She went to the nearest chair to the door and perched on it, her hands clutching her purse on her lap, her eyes darted nervously around the room.

Tomlinson sat beside her and patted her knee, his eyes boring into Jim's who had escorted them in and who now stood at the door clearly barring any escape. You could see how much the agent wanted to tear Jim limb from limb, but since Jim outweighed him, you could also see how Tomlinson was employing good sense by staying in his seat.

I was particularly interested in whether or not Janice would show up, and when she did a few minutes later, like the others, she looked around in confusion and distrust.

"Take a seat, Miss Gruntz," I said. "This shouldn't take long. And then all but one of you can be on your way."

"What is the meaning of this?" she asked shrilly.

Like Millie, she was clutching her handbag to her chest.

"Sit down, Janice," Jim said in that crooning voice of his.

I knew he was aware that Janice had taken a shine to him. She looked at him, her eyes glowing with trust, then took a seat between Tomlinson and Don Berford.

By this time, Tomlinson's knee was bouncing up and down rapidly as he chewed a fingernail. Berford was staring hard at the table with the folders I'd set on it, his lips pursed tightly. Shadows crept into the corners of the room, accentuating the already high tensions. I scanned each suspect one by one, probing for any new insight that might change my mind from what I thought I now knew about the identity of the killer. Beside me, Jim radiated a calming yet commanding presence.

"Well?" Berford said. "What are we waiting for?"

"One more person," I said.

I glanced at Jim. Had Murphy decided not to come? Just then I heard a someone enter the entrance of the club. Within seconds, Patrick Murphy appeared in the doorway of the small room, his dark wavy hair having been tossed around his face by the wind outside. He nodded a solemn greeting to me and Jim before taking a seat with his arms crossed, a muscle ticking in his clenched jaw.

"I've called you all here tonight," I said in my most authoritative announcer voice, "to reveal the identity of Celeste Latour's killer."

I scanned each of their faces, lingering on their expressions. Some of them seemed nervous—mostly Millie and Janice—some defiant—Tomlinson and Berford, and some just weary—Murphy. One of these people was responsible for Celeste Latour's death and now that I had them in front of me, I was more convinced than ever that I knew exactly who that was.

If I was at all unsure before, I was absolutely sure now.

"This is preposterous," Berford said snorting derisively. "Who do you think you are, Philip Marlowe?"

"Let's start with you, Mr. Berford," I said.

He sat up straight and glanced around him.

"This is a monkey trial," he said. "The police have already discounted my involvement."

He continued to look around as though expecting someone to confirm this for him. When I walked over to him, I saw a bead of perspiration dribble down his forehead.

"I overheard you conspiring with Gerald Tomlinson," I said. "It sounded like you were trying to get free of your wife."

Tomlinson jumped to his feet.

"Don't bring me into this!" he said.

"You're already in this," Jim said. "Sit down and shut up until we get to you."

Tomlinson looked around and slowly sank back again in his chair. I knew how badly he needed that letter back that revealed he'd been fired by Celeste on the day she died. I watched his eyes as they went to the stack of files Jim and I had placed on the table.

I turned back to Berford. "Mr. Berford?"

"I already told you," he said. "That was about a script that Celeste had signed on for that wasn't good for her career."

"You really wanted out of that movie contract, didn't you?" I asked.

"I wouldn't kill her for it!" he said. "Besides, what good would killing her have done?"

"Well, your prenup prevents you from getting any money from the dissolution of the marriage," I said walking over to the table and picking up a folder. "But you stand to inherit everything if your wife dies before you."

Berford looked at me in absolute astonishment. I gave it a beat and then turned to Jim.

"I don't think he knew," I said.

"Unless he's a better actor than his wife," Jim said.

"I...I inherit?" Berford stuttered.

"Let's put a pin in that, shall we?" I said, turning away and directing my attention to Millie who was trembling so hard I tried to imagine if she could be somehow willing herself to do it.

"Miss Ross," I said. "You admitted to me that you hated Celeste."

Millie's eyes widened and she looked around as if the others were her jury and she needed to appeal to them.

"That's...that's not true," she said.

"I've got a waitress at The Rusty Spoon who is willing to testify that she overheard you say it to me."

"Yes, okay, I said it," Millie said, her eyes wild as she hugged her purse even more tightly to her chest and began to rock. "But I didn't kill her!"

"But you could've," I said. "You had the means, didn't you?"

Millie didn't answer, just stared down at her bitten nails.

"Who here knows of your medical condition?" I asked her.

She shook her head. I looked at the three men and one woman sitting before me.

"I know *you* knew, Mr. Berford," I said turning to Don Berford. "You were the one who told us about it." I turned to Murphy. "And of course, I'm sure Celeste would tell her bodyguard about it. That seems pertinent information her security should have."

Murphy nodded his head. "Yeah, she told me."

I turned back to Tomlinson and Janice. "Well?"

"Okay, yes," Tomlinson said. "Millie and I are friends. So, of course, I knew."

"Okay," I said. "Miss Gruntz?"

Janice shook her head.

"I don't know what you're talking about."

"I'm talking about the daily dose of digitalis that Miss Ross takes to treat a heart ailment. A dose much like the one your own mother takes. A medicine that is fatal if taken inappropriately. A medicine that you have daily access to, Miss Gruntz, regardless of whether you knew about Miss Ross's dependence on it."

Janice paled, fear flashing across her face before she collected herself.

"You have no proof of anything," she said. But her voice trembled.

I leaned in, my eyes boring into hers.

"That's just it, Miss Gruntz," I said. "I actually do."

40

I have to say that what I just did there was an age-old trick that interrogators have been using for a long time. Unless the person is actually innocent, it usually works to sufficiently rattle the person attempting to prevaricate. In this case, since I didn't believe Janice killed her sister, it was someone else I wanted to unnerve, someone who was listening to me state that I had proof of who killed Celeste Latour.

"I am telling you the truth," Janice said, blinking rapidly and looking from me to Jim and back again. "I didn't get a chance to even talk to my sister that night."

"Maybe talking wasn't your intention," I said.

"I didn't kill her!" she said hotly. "I didn't want her dead! I wanted her sorry! How does me going to prison for murder help anything?"

"Good point," I said. "I'd say your motive is the weakest of all. Which is why I can tell you now, Miss Gruntz, that you were lured here under false pretenses. I don't have a letter from your sister threatening to make public anything about you possibly having killed her."

"What?!" Janice said, her mouth open wide in outrage.

I turned to Berford.

"And as far as I know, your wife never kept a diary, so you're in the clear too, Don."

"Wait a minute!" Berford sputtered. "There's no diary?"

"That's right," I said. "I apologize for any embarrassment my little ruse might have caused you."

If not for the fact that he'd just found out he was inheriting a fortune, I think Berford would have been much more irate about being lured here under the threat of having a ruinous rumor exposed to the world. As it was, he jumped to his feet.

"So we're done?" he asked.

"You and Miss Gruntz are," I said, glancing at Jim who shrugged and went to open the door for them.

"I should report you to the police," Berford said as he made his way past the others on his way toward the door.

"I definitely intend to report you!" Janice huffed as she hurried out behind him.

Once they were gone, I turned to the three still sitting, my heart pounding with anticipation since the moment of reveal was now upon us. I turned to Millie.

"You're in the clear, too, Millie," I said. "I'm sorry to have put you through this but it was necessary."

Millie covered her face with her hands. Tomlinson put an arm protectively around her and addressed me angrily.

"If you are about to say that *I* killed Celeste," he snarled, his face beet red, "I can tell you right now that I'd already found a whole new roster of clients, so getting fired from a star who was past her prime was not something that would drive me to kill!"

"Wow," I said. "I'm glad to hear that, Mr. Tomlinson. Congratulations on the new clients. And thank you for coming tonight. Honestly, you were never a serious suspect, but we needed to have the whole gang here tonight. You and Miss Ross are free to go."

I turned to Patrick Murphy.

"I have to say I really enjoyed meeting your wife the other day, Officer Murphy. And I appreciate you coming tonight too, especially because I never had anything to tie you to the murder."

"Glad I could help," he said with a shrug.

"Which is why it makes this all the more egregious," I said, "when I realized that it was in fact you who killed Celeste Latour."

Millie sucked in a breath loudly. But Murphy stayed seated, a slow smile drawing on his face as he regarded me.

"How in the world did you get there?" he said finally.

"Pretty easily," I said. "In the end."

"We checked your alibi," Jim said. "The manager of the club said the men's room was disabled that night. You didn't use it. You lied."

"And *why* would you have lied?" I said as I walked over to the table. "Is it because you were angry at how your old girlfriend Cece dropped you and then went on to become rich and famous? I heard from one of the waitresses at the club that when she interviewed you for the job of bodyguard, she didn't even know who you were at first. That must have hurt. Does your wife know? Or was that even your wife we met?"

"I love my wife and the kiddies."

Murphy said it flatly and without emotion.

"Okay, well, I guess Katie can hardly compare to a famous movie star," I said.

"That bitch made promises to me," Murphy said angrily.

"I spent the last ten years reading fan magazines about her and all her movie star boyfriends."

"I get it. That would be tough. And then there was the new movie."

"So, you know about that? Yeah, she showed it to me. She played the mother but the story was about some shlub who gets left behind while his high school girlfriend goes on to fame and fortune. I could just imagine all my buddies —the whole police department—getting a good laugh at that when the movie came out."

"So you killed her."

"It's not how I wanted it to happen," he said.

"Poison a bit too passive for you?" Jim asked.

Murphy snapped his head around to answer him.

"She deserved to be throttled to death," he said.

"But I guess that would be a little tricky since you only saw her in public," I said. "The evidence was all there—the new movie, the easy access to Millie's pills, and of course near constant opportunity."

"Yeah, except a smart dame like you probably knows that circumstantial evidence won't stand up in court," Murphy said with a sneer.

"Oh, I know," I said, picking up a piece of paper from the table and holding it up. "Which is why we went through your locker tonight while you were on patrol looking for evidence of what I suspected and we found this."

I waved the letter in the air and watched his face freeze in shock and horror.

"It makes for fascinating reading," I said, turning to Millie and Tomlinson. "It's basically a rough draft of a letter in Officer Murphy's handwriting addressed to someone named Cece saying how her days were numbered." I turned back to Murphy.

"You're quite the one for the cliché, I must say, Officer Murphy. You were overheard saying you were going to *fix her wagon* and you nearly got me and Jim to believe it was just a playful joke between the two of you. Nearly."

Murphy stood up and pulled out his service revolver.

"I'll take that letter," he said.

I should've expected him to come armed.

"What's happening?" Tomlinson said, putting an arm around Millie who was now trembling so hard she was practically shaking the whole line of chairs.

I handed Murphy the letter.

"You know that's just a copy, right?" I said. "I've got the original somewhere safe."

"I'm pretty sure the original dies with you," Murphy said with a laugh.

I felt Jim move from behind me and I knew he had every intention of taking the first bullet. I stepped in front of him and felt his hand go to my waist to move me aside.

"If you intend to use your own service weapon tonight, Officer Murphy," I said, "you better hope for a good head start because I don't think you can explain four dead bodies. Especially since we're all unarmed."

He grinned.

"I wasn't going to shoot you, darling," he said. "I was going to leave you alive and well."

I didn't dare look at Jim during all this. I knew he carried a knife, but I prayed he wouldn't attack Murphy. Nothing beats a gun in a gun fight. If Murphy intended to lock us up in the room while he fled, we needed to just let it happen. We would get out eventually and he would be captured. There was no point in Jim taking a bullet for no reason.

It wasn't ideal. I'd had hopes of putting Murphy in handcuffs and marching him to the police station, but this was still workable. I wasn't worried, at least not until I watched Murphy walk backwards to the door, his gun on us, his grin growing wider. He stopped at the door and leaned down to pick something up while keeping the gun aimed at us.

What happened next happened so quickly I wasn't sure I really saw what I saw.

Murphy picked up a large hemp bag that he must have dropped just outside the private room door when he'd come in. In one movement, he jerked open the tie that held it shut and tossed the bag into the room before slamming the door behind him.

"What the hell?" Tomlinson said as he moved toward the door.

Just about the same time that Millie began to scream.

41

Millie's scream pierced the air as the burlap sack began emptying of its contents—a writhing mass of venomous cottonmouth snakes. Too many to count immediately. The serpents slithered out in every direction across the floor.

Screams of raw terror filled the air as Millie and Tomlinson scrambled to climb up and away from the snakes. Even in the dim lighting I could see their shiny scales glistening as they slithered across the wooden floor. Tomlinson frantically jumped away from a snake which had coiled with its head raised high in threat mode to strike his leg.

"Don't kick at them!" I screamed. "Back away!"

As chaos erupted in the room, Millie's screams seemed to agitate the snakes further and their movements becoming more frenzied. I didn't have time to even glance at Jim. My eyes were everywhere at once because that's where the snakes were. I tried to remember if cottonmouths were afraid of people or abnormally aggressive. Not that it mattered because these had already been riled up by being bagged together before being dumped on the floor with big human animals looming over them.

I felt the sweat pour off me. Several of the snakes were stretched out immobile on the floor. Others were coiled up with their mouths widely open in their trademark threat display to reveal the white interior from which they got their name. I raised my voice to be heard over Millie's screams.

"Nobody make any sudden movement," I shouted as I climbed onto the center table. "Snakes can sense vibrations and movement will only frighten and agitate them."

"Help me! Help me!" Millie whimpered two snakes writhed beneath her chair.

Another large cottonmouth uncoiled itself rapidly, then darted straight towards Tomlinson with lightning speed. Its body was a single thick rope of interlocking muscle and scale, rippling with power. Tomlinson screamed and jumped back on the chair as he watched another of the vipers rear up before him. He kicked at it and the serpent struck, hitting his shoe and then it struck again. Tomlinson stood up on his chair, then screamed as he leaned backward precariously.

I looked around me in desperation. Behind me was a small bar of basic spirits. Without looking at the labels, I snatched up three bottles of vodka and threw them into the mass of snakes. The bottles broke, splashing on snakes and spreading liquid all across the floor. Instantly, the snakes reacted as a ball of writhing frenzy.

"Jim! A match!" I screamed. "Throw a match!"

Jim whipped out his lighter, his face a mask of focused intent despite the danger all around him. He ignited the lighter and held it to a ripped in two book of matches before tossing them into the puddles of pure ethanol on and around the snakes. Immediately, a bright fire flared up as the snakes reacted with writhing fury. I felt my stomach revolt at the smell of frying chicken in the room.

"Time to move, people!" Jim shouted as we watched the few surviving snakes crawl off in search of dark corners in the room.

His deep commanding tone did more than all my words before him had done. Millie still whimpered but she was no longer screaming. Tomlinson was still standing on a chair but no longer kicking at anything that got near him. There were large patches of fire on the floor where the vodka had spilled but they were quickly burning out. I didn't see any snakes near them.

"There's a clear path to the door," Jim said calmly. "Take it slowly, one step at a time."

"I can't!" Millie screeched. "I can't! Gerry, help me!"

"Just sit tight," Jim said to her. "I'll carry you."

"No, I'll do it," Tomlinson said in a shaky voice.

I was impressed. Well, mostly, I was terrified. Later, if I survived, I knew I'd be impressed with Tomlinson saying he'd carry Millie. With Jim directing us in calm, comforting tones, we all began to control our rapid breathing and slowly relax our death grips on whatever surfaces we were clinging to.

"Okay, everyone," Jim said, as he tentatively lowered one foot onto the floor from the chair he'd been standing on. "On my mark...slowly and carefully. Go slow. Watch where you put your foot. Head for the door."

Slowly, painstakingly, we all began moving with deliberate care as if wading through water. The exit door was less than twenty feet away, and no snakes in a direct line to it. Tomlinson went first, with Millie gripping his arm tightly, letting him lead her out step by torturous step. I was behind them, with Jim bringing up the rear.

Out of the corner of my eye, I saw movement, but I stayed focused on the door, now only a few feet away. I heard the unmistakable sound of a snake striking, and my stomach tightened. But it was striking against one of its own. The urge to run, to get this horrible nightmare over with was nearly overwhelming. But I couldn't be the one to break and run. Time seemed to stand still as I took another step toward the door, terrified that my legs were about to give out on me. I felt Jim's hand on my back and immediately felt reassured. His touch said *take a breath, don't rush it*. I let out a long breath. Slowly, we began to move again toward the door.

The door loomed up in front of us and I found myself praying that Murphy hadn't bothered to lock it. Surely, he would have assumed he'd taken care of us and there was no need to bother? I watched with my heart in my throat as Tomlinson reached out and turned the knob.

It didn't open.

Jim was past me in two strides, his shoulder smashing into the door. Millie screamed as Tomlinson pushed past Jim, dragging her with him. I couldn't help myself then and I bolted through the doorway as well. I heard the snakes activate behind me but it was all over by then.

We ran through the club, out the front door into the night air and down the alley that led to the main street, all of us shaking with gratitude and relief.

42

Millie and Tomlinson immediately fell into each other's arms where Millie began weeping again, this time with tears of joy and relief. Jim put his arm around me for support and for a minute there I really needed it. I hate snakes. I've always hated them. The thought that *that* was how I was going to die had been a thought I'd had to work particularly hard to vanquish when I was surrounded by them. Tomlinson was the first to break the silence. He turned to Jim.

"The letter you promised?" he said sternly, holding out his hand. "Since I assume you now know I didn't kill Celeste."

"Yeah, sorry about that, pal," Jim said with a shrug. "I left it back there. You're welcome to go get it."

Tomlinson went red in the face as he glanced back at the door of the Cottonmouth Club—now quite literally that.

"It doesn't matter," I said to him. "Once we tell the police what happened tonight, they won't see that letter as incriminating."

That seemed to mollify him. Millie wiped her tears and

stepped over to me, her eyes glittering with tears and fury. She lifted her hand suddenly me but Jim instantly caught her hand before she could slap me. She jerked away from him, her eyes still on me.

"I can't believe you put us through that," she said. "We were innocent but that was irrelevant. You're a monster."

I flushed because I knew she was right, but Jim wasn't having it.

"She's fighting for her life, Miss Ross," he said tartly. "If you had to go through an uncomfortable night to clear the name of an innocent person, then so be it. Surely, you're not that petty?"

I could see his words had an effect on her. She was still upset but she'd forgotten that without flushing out the real killer, I was the one who would pay the price for a crime I didn't commit.

"Take me home, Gerald," she said, turning away in lieu of an apology.

Jim and I watched them go. The thick night air hung heavily, nearly smothering us. Somewhere, one street over I hear a car with a loud muffler droning.

"Well," he said. "Now what? Head to the police station?"

"I'm not sure," I said. "We've given Murphy Intel about the others that he could use to deflect attention from himself."

"I thought about that."

"We weren't specific about the homosexuality claim for Don Berford," I said as we turned to walk where we'd parked his car. "Nor did he know about Tomlinson's incriminating letter."

"But we basically revealed that Millie Ross had no alibi for the night, and she had possession of the same drug that killed the victim."

"Janice too," I said. "But won't they all support what we all heard tonight? I mean Murphy confessed and Millie and Tomlinson heard it."

Jim rubbed a hand across his face and then looked at his watch.

"We're not done tonight, are we?" I said.

He looked at me and then back at the Cottonmouth Club.

"We found out who killed Celeste Latour," he said. "But we didn't catch him."

"Do you think he's still in town?"

"Why wouldn't he be? He thinks he just eliminated the four people who knew he committed murder."

A feeling of dread came over me.

"Not quite," I said. "Berford and Janice may not have stuck around to hear Murphy confess, but the field was sufficiently narrowed by the time they left. They have to know it was one of those three. I'm not sure Murphy will be comfortable with those odds."

Jim gave me the same sick look I was feeling in my gut.

"You're right," he said. "But do we try to find Janice or Berford first?"

I stared at him and realized that if we guessed wrong, someone—either Janice or Berford—was going to die tonight at the hands of a brutal and vindictive Irish police officer.

43

The rumble of Jim's Model T cut through the night as we pulled away from the curb. I settled into the passenger seat. The mahogany dashboard and fittings facing me reflected light from the passing streetlamps.

I thought about flipping a coin to decide who to go after first—Berford or Janice—but in the end I thought Murphy would go for the easiest target first. That meant Janice.

"Shouldn't we tell Sam what we're doing?" Jim asked.

"Sam doesn't listen to me," I said. "And he's too jealous of you to be sensible."

Smoke from Jim's cigarette curled in the air as we drove to Janice's neighborhood. I rolled down my window and looked out into the night, too wound up and exhausted to register Jim's reaction to that statement. It seemed impossible that it had only been four hours since he'd kissed me in the park.

We arrived at Janice's apartment building, but the street was quiet. The fact that Murphy's car was nowhere to be seen did not bode well for our chances of finding her. Either we were wrong about which one Murphy decided to go after first, or we were too late.

We climbed out of the car and hurried to her building and then to her apartment where Jim pounded on the door. There was no answer. We both shouted—sufficient to wake up the rest of the building. But Janice's apartment remained quiet.

We'd guessed wrong.

We turned and sprinted back to the car.

"Now what?" I asked breathlessly as I climbed in and fumbled for a seatbelt I would not find.

"Is it too late for her to visit her mother?" Jim asked.

Just the thought of that murderous Murphy at the Magnolia Manor with all those vulnerable people made me tremble. I glanced at my watch. It was after four o'clock in the morning. Surely it was too early for Janice to be visiting her mother? But where else would she go?

Suddenly I got an image in my mind of Janice and Don Berford exchanging knowing gazes. It was nothing obvious and not immediately amorous. But neither was it the sort of look two acquaintances might give each other. That's when it occurred to me again of how much Janice looked like her sister.

Was it possible that Berford was having an affair with Celeste's sister? Even if he wasn't, what if he was just drawn to her? Now that Celeste was out of the way and money wasn't an issue...

"I think Janice is with Berford at his hotel," I said.

"You think Berford and Janice are a couple?" Jim frowned. "I didn't see that."

"I don't think there was anything to see before tonight," I said. "But I'll bet they're together."

A look of grim understanding passed over his face.

"We need to hurry," he said.

This time there was no need for subterfuge or hiding in the shrubbery. Jim parked at the curb and we bolted for the front door of the Marshall House. We raced inside, unmindful of the shouts from the concierge who of course had already seen us both once earlier tonight racing through the lobby. As with Tomlinson, we knew which room was Don Berford's and we made a beeline for it. We arrived at his door, panting. This time, Jim didn't bother with his lockpicking tools. He put his shoulder to the door and heaved it open with a mighty crash.

The scene before us was one of complete turmoil. Furniture was overturned, lamps and framed prints smashed on the floor. Bloody footprints stained the carpet. Sheets were ripped from the bed, pillows strewn about, with feathers floating through the air like snowflakes, evidence of a violent struggle.

"This is not good," Jim said as we looked at the destroyed hotel room.

"Perfume," I said suddenly. "I smell Janice's perfume. She was here." I turned to Jim with mounting dread. "They're together."

"They can't have been gone long," Jim said.

I felt a tightness bloom in my chest as I realized that Don and Janice's lives likely hung in the balance for a matter of minutes now. We turned and ran back downstairs past the concierge who was on the phone—hopefully to the police although he was probably calling them on me and Jim. We ran outside and saw what we should've seen if we hadn't been so focused on getting inside.

Murphy's police car was sitting on the dark street. As soon as we saw it, the cruiser's taillights illuminated.

"There he is!" I said.

Jim and I bolted for the car when suddenly Jim grabbed me and pulled me out of the street to make way for a fire engine speeding past. I'd been so caught up at the sight of Murphy's car that I hadn't even heard the sirens. I felt myself trembling in Jim's hands as I realized that the sky seemed significantly brighter than it should have for this time of night. I turned to look behind us. I did a double take as nausea erupted in my gut.

The horizon was aglow with fire.

44

The Cottonmouth Club was on fire.

I don't know why I didn't think of it before, but *of course* Murphy would need to erase all evidence of his involvement at the club tonight—especially if that evidence included four bodies in a locked room killed by snake bites. Either that or the puddles of fire we'd set to fight off the snakes had reignited once we left.

But whatever the reason, the burning speakeasy was the perfect diversion for Murphy while he got rid of the two people I had to assume were locked in his car trunk. If only DNA analysis existed back in this time! There was no way he would get away with hauling Don and Janice around in his car trunk and not be found out! But this was 1924. And the only way he was going to be caught today was if Jim and I caught him.

We ran to Jim's car and hopped in, but as he cranked it, nothing happened.

"What is it?" I asked, my voice thready with dread. "Why won't it start?"

"Damn it," Jim said slamming his open hand against the steering wheel.

I looked around the street at the other cars parked there.

"Do you know how to hot-wire a car?" I asked.

He narrowed his eyes at me.

"How do you even know that term? Never mind. Yeah, yeah. Give me a second."

Murphy was already maneuvering his car down the road and headed out of town, probably to someplace where he could bury the bodies. I prayed he hadn't yet dispatched the pair.

"There!" I said, pointing at an older Model T parked on the street a half block behind Jim's car.

Jim and I jumped out and hurried toward the car.

"Beats a horse and buggy," he said as he opened the door and slid into the driver's seat. "Keep watch!"

I turned and kept an eye on the activity on the street, but I needn't have worried. The street had come alive with people running around shouting as yet another fire truck went wailing down the street toward the Cottonmouth Club. Even from where I stood next to the car, I could see the speakeasy was engulfed in flames. Suddenly, I felt the car roar to life.

"Get in!" Jim shouted.

I knew from experience there would be no seatbelts, nor anything rounded or padded on the interior. That was fine when I was traveling at a stately fifteen miles an hour but as Jim revved the motor and peeled away from the curb, I knew that even a fender-bender at the lowest possible speed would put us both in the hospital—if we were lucky.

"Do you think he's already killed them?" I shouted over the noisy engine as Jim barreled out of town, dodging a couple of curious onlookers headed for the site of the fire.

"I don't know," he said. "He doesn't know we survived the snakes so he's probably not in a mad hurry just yet unless he saw us run into the hotel. But he'll still try to silence any witnesses."

I prayed that for the very reason Jim believed—that Murphy felt he was in no real hurry tonight—that we would have the necessary edge. As soon as we left the city environs behind us, we spotted the rear lights of a car sixty yards ahead of us.

"There he is!" I shouted. "Floor it!"

I'm not sure what the plan was beyond catching up with Murphy and making sure he didn't have time to stop and deal with the contents of his trunk. Our borrowed car rattled and shook at this speed and then began to fish tail. My heart was pounding in my chest, and I stifled a scream as we neared the back end of Murphy's car in front of us.

"He's seen us!" I shouted.

I could see from the interior light of the car ahead that Murphy was watching us in his rear-view mirror. I couldn't imagine what his next move might be which is why I was unprepared for the scream of the bullet ripping through the sun visor over my head.

"Get down!" Jim shouted.

I immediately ducked and heard two more bullets rake the car. Suddenly Jim cried out. I looked over at him to see him gripping his arm and trying to drive with one hand.

"You're hit!" I said.

We were slowing down as Jim began to lose control of the vehicle.

"Jim! Where are you hit?" I shouted as I grabbed the wheel.

He slumped against me as the car slowed to a stop. I twisted the wheel to keep it from going off the road into a high ditch beside us. Hurriedly with my hands shaking, I put the car in park and then pulled Jim away from the steering wheel.

"I'm okay," he moaned.

But he wasn't. He wasn't even lucid. He helped me get him out of the driver's seat. I locked the passenger side door and leaned him up against it. A part of me wanted to drive him straight to the hospital but the other part of me knew that I was the only thing standing between a cold shallow grave and life for Don and Janice.

"You're going to be okay," I said to Jim as I climbed into the driver's seat.

I put the car into drive and gave it gas as I maneuvered off the verge and back onto the road. It had started to rain and between that and the moonless night, it was almost impossible to see. I fumbled for the windshield wipers and bit the inside of my mouth as I gunned the car down the road, trying to see past the rain for the brake lights ahead of me.

I drove for several long moments. But there was nothing.

Could Murphy have taken a side road? I thought in a panic. Maybe he pulled off the road and turned his lights off? I cursed the fact that I was driving blind in just about every sense. Suddenly, I sailed past what looked like a dark shape parked off the road. The minute I was past, its headlights came on and within seconds, he was behind me. I looked in the rearview window. It was him.

A crushing jab of fear raced through me. I don't know how, but I knew he was going to ram me long seconds before I felt the impact as Murphy's drove into the back of my car. Instantly, the steering wheel flew out of my hands and we swerved recklessly across the wet road. I scrambled to grab the wheel again, but I was off the road now, mowing down bushes, boulders, highway signs. Through it all, I knew that maniac was still behind me, still coming for me.

I gripped the wheel and depressed the accelerator as far as I could press it, the headlights from Murphy's car bouncing erratically behind me. I knew he had a gun. Stopping for a showdown was out of the question. I tried to imagine what his goal was. Then I switched gears and tried to imagine what he was expecting *me* to do.

Because whatever that was, I needed to make sure I did the opposite.

Up ahead I saw the tree line that I had been roughly using as a guide had vanished. My heart pounded as I tried to imagine what that could mean.

In a moment of cold dread, I realized that either I was heading into a pasture—in which case sooner or later a barbed wire fence was about to stop me.

Or I was racing toward a cliff.

45

There was no time to think. I assumed Murphy knew the area better than I did. He knew what it was I was driving toward. I could take my chances with him and his gun or with gravity as my car plummeted to a stony and abrupt end.

I chose the latter and gunned it. The car roared ahead by several yards. My eyes went again to the horizon where the trees should be, and then back at Murphy. I'd caught him by surprise. He hadn't expected me to race toward my own death. He came on in relentless pursuit.

"Cover your head!" I shouted at Jim. "Cover your head!"

At the last moment, I spun the steering wheel hard. The car slewed violently sideways until it stopped at a ninety-degree angle blocking Murphy as he barreled down the dirt road after me. I instantly put myself into the time-honored crash position, grabbing my head and knees and praying. I didn't have time to see how Murphy reacted just before hitting me broadside, but I heard his brakes squealing as he slammed onto them.

Too late.

As he t-boned us there was a thunderous crash that shook me to my core and wrenched me out of my seat. More than that was the sudden movement as the car spun violently before falling over on its side, my body going with it like a ragdoll's. Sharp metal protuberances of the car's interior ripped into me. I felt my head smash into the window which exploded around me like a throbbing marquee of stars. My whole world was nothing but pain and the sound of grinding metal and shattering glass.

When the car finally stopped moving, I felt my very brain humming like a locomotive coming down the track. Blood ran into my eyes, and I heard Jim cough weakly. Through a haze of pain, I turned to see him, covered in lacerations, still clutching his injured arm. I wiped the blood from my face and my arm screamed in agony when I did.

"Jim?" I said, my voice strangled by my split and bruised lips. "Jim!"

"I'm here," he said dully, his voice laced with pain.

He was alive. I looked around and suddenly the sharp stench of gasoline filled my nostrils along with the acrid smell of burning rubber and metal. I turned my head to see the front of Murphy's car rammed up against a tree. After hitting us and knocking us out of the way, his car had continued on until it hit the tree. I saw his car's hood was buckled with smoke pouring out from it. Murphy was collapsed over the steering wheel, his head bowed as if in prayer.

I needed to get Jim out and away from the smell of this gas. I climbed out of the backseat where I'd landed from the impact of the crash, gingerly feeling my way but trying to hurry too. I leaned across Jim and opened his passenger side door and gently pushed him out onto the grass. I heard him moan when he hit the ground. I was sorry about that, but it couldn't be helped. I followed after him and grabbed him by the arm to pull him. He yelled and pushed me away, so I tried the other arm.

"Come on, Jim," I said. "I have to get you away from the car before it blows."

He roused himself enough to half crawl with me as I tugged him to a nearby tree. I left him there and ran to Murphy's car. I went to the trunk and opened it with its handle. Janice and Don had been about as far away from the point of impact as they could be, but they were still badly shaken. Blood streamed down Don's face and both of them stared at me with large, terrified eyes.

"Get out!" I shouted. "Hurry! The car is going to explode!"

I knew we had only seconds. If that. But my words triggered in them the same terror I was feeling. They clamored out of the trunk and ran stumbling to where Jim lay. I turned back to see Murphy in the driver's seat of his car. He lifted his head and looked at me. I could see in his eyes that he knew what was happening. For one mad moment I thought he was going to apologize or ask for my understanding.

Instead, he pulled out his service revolver and leveled it at me.

I was so astonished, that I just stood there staring as the rain came down harder. The moment felt like a dream. A really bad dream, but one that didn't feel as if I had any actual control over it. In the end, I'll never know if he'd have shot me or if I would've snapped out of it and dived for cover in the nick of time. Neither of those things happened, because right then, the earth rumbled in time with an explosion as the car Murphy sat in blew up knocking me off my feet.

I lay on the ground, vibrating in pain and deaf to all noise. Debris from the car and Murphy himself peppered the earth around me in a macabre shower. I was not immediately sure what had just happened. But when the smoke cleared, one thing I knew was that Officer Patrick Murphy would not be terrorizing anyone ever again.

46

The cool early autumn air was perfumed with the scent of late season flowers as I stepped out into the garden behind my townhouse. It was four days after the night of the car accident which was now just a blur of tears and relief and pain. Both Don Berford and Janice Gruntz had been appropriately grateful at being rescued. We heard their hair-raising story of being dragged by Patrick Murphy to the trunk of his car, and of course we knew the rest after that. When they heard about the snakes back at the Cottonmouth Club, they were duly horrified. And I think it made their own ordeal a tiny bit less harrowing. I'm not sure which I'd choose: being attacked by a swarm of venomous snakes or being shoved in a trunk by a murderous madman.

Jim and I both ended up in the hospital that night: him with a gunshot wound that had thankfully hit nothing important, me with a hairline fractured ulna, and both of us with assorted scrapes and bruises. Trust me, the advances that car manufacturers have made in my time to keep the interior of cars safe is nothing short of miraculous. Forget the lack of seat belts, everything in that Model T was pointy and lethally jagged and that was *before* the accident, since afterward the car interior essentially got turned into scrap metal.

A lazy hum rose from the garden, mostly the sound of insects and birds still alive and well in Savannah in October —far from the noise of the city street just beyond the garden walls. I glanced at my wristwatch. You'd think I wouldn't have to wait for Sam after solving his case for him. Again. But I suppose I should be grateful he didn't insist on this final debrief down at the police station. Talking to me here in the comfort of my own garden was probably his way of throwing me a bone.

I have to say that in the aftermath of everything that went down Sam hasn't been terrible, all things considered. He even visited me during my one night in the hospital, and he did seem somewhat contrite when he heard that it was his own officer who killed Celeste Latour. But one thing I've learned from this historical time is that the men here don't do *mea culpa* very well. He spent most of his visit with me in the hospital telling me how I was no longer considered a suspect and how he'd been promised a promotion for wrapping things up so quickly.

I was pretty shocked at his callous attitude and I have to say right then and there my own words came back to haunt me when I remembered how I'd wanted to solve this murder to make Sam proud of me and make him look good to his superiors. I'm ashamed that I ever thought that. Because the man wasn't worthy of it. It occurred to me I should mention this new insight to Mary one of these days since she was the one who had been saying the very same thing to me all along.

I'd wanted to tell Sam during that hospital visit that the

only thing *he'd* done to solve the case was to arrest the wrong person who was then motivated to do the actual detective work to find the real killer. But I didn't. My arm wasn't the only thing that was healing during this time. My broken heart was trying to mend too. I asked him if he'd been in to see Jim who was hurt much worse than I was, but he said he was too busy. Then I told him that my mother died, and I would be leaving town to settle her estate and he blurted out the most ill-timed, tone-deaf statement I could possibly ever imagine hearing.

"I'm getting married."

I think I just stared at him, my arm throbbing, wondering if I could possibly feel any worse.

"Congratulations," I managed to say.

"Thanks. It's happening quickly because it took us both by surprise. She's a great gal."

I really didn't want all the gory details and he clearly didn't want to spend any more time with me in the hospital. Now that I think of it, this was the first time in a long time when what we both wanted seemed to actually coincide.

"Miss Georgia?"

I looked up to see Ruby standing in the French doors that led inside the townhouse. She was dressed in a simple day dress and was drying her hands on a kitchen towel. I'd walked straight over to the diner on my way home from the hospital and offered her and her husband jobs as my live-in cook and handyman. After she'd stopped crying, she agreed. She'd only been here two days and already I've eaten better than I ever have in my life. Bert—a burly and very jolly one-armed man—has fixed two shutters, a plumbing problem and a large hole in the chimney.

"Please just call me Georgia," I said as I turned to her.

"Yes'm," she said. "Detective Bohannon done called and said he can't make it today."

I turned away and found that, amazingly, I was relieved. The last thing I wanted to do was hear more about how he'd solved the case on his own. Or the happy preparations for his upcoming wedding.

"Okay, thanks, Ruby," I said.

"And Mister Jim is here," she said.

I was on my feet immediately, but Jim appeared from behind Ruby. He still wore a sling to support the arm where he'd been shot, and he looked tired, but otherwise he looked wonderful.

"This is a nice surprise," I said as he stepped into the garden while Ruby went back in the kitchen. "Can you stay for supper?"

"If you'll have me."

He settled on the Adirondack chair opposite mine and Libby tried to leap into his lap.

"How are you feeling?" I asked.

"Better hour by hour," he said.

"I need to thank you for all the help you—"

He held up his good hand.

"Stop it, Georgia," he said sternly. "You know why I did it. You know how I feel about you."

I smiled in spite of myself. This was not the age for over-the-top pronouncements of love. So I appreciated the declaration.

"I have feelings for you too, Jim."

"If you need me to fight Sam to win you, you'll have to wait until I'm back on my feet. But I'm pretty sure I can take him."

"Funny guy," I said with a grin. "No fighting. You'll win me all on your own."

He looked into my eyes, his gaze strong and hopeful.

"Do you mean that?" he asked.

"I tell you what," I said. "Let's have a wonderful home cooked meal by my new cook and friend Ruby James and then why don't you and I retire upstairs for some very gentle but effective physical therapy?"

His eyes widened in shock and moments later when Ruby called us in to dinner, he practically knocked over his chair getting out of it. Later, when we were alone, I found him exactly as I knew he'd be—sensitive, gentle and intuitive. A part of me wanted to be in his arms as a way to say thank you for the loving friendship he'd shown me. I knew what we were doing tonight wasn't totally fair to him. My head still wasn't straight about how I felt. Not with Sam so recently dethroned from my heart's desire. I'm not sure what Jim thought about what we did tonight either, beyond simple delight at getting lucky. No, I take that back. I'm pretty sure he saw tonight as a stepping-stone to something more.

And who knows? Maybe it was.

Right now, I couldn't think of that.

Afterward, he held me with his good arm and looked into my eyes, his face happy and aglow. I kissed him on the mouth and then very gently told him who I really was.

47

I have to say Jim didn't stay long after that.

I walked with him in my fluffy Kohls robe and flip flops to the foyer. Bert was up and escorted Jim—who never looked back—the rest of the way out, locking up after him. I thanked Bert, told him to go to bed, and went back upstairs myself where, amazingly I slept well for the first time in months.

The next morning, Libby and I met Mary at Colonial Park where she arrived with a hamper of fried chicken and potato salad. It was too damp from a recent rain to sit on a blanket on the ground, so we settled for the benches, but it was still nice. Mary knew I was going back to 2024, of course. She would be taking Libby from me after our lunch. She also knew I intended to come back.

"How's your arm?" she asked as she scooped potato salad onto a plate.

"It was only a hairline fracture," I said. "I need to remember to bring more ibuprofen back with me. Like a truckload since I don't know when I'll go back to the future."

I'd told her about the movie with that same name, but

she didn't really get how it was funny. Pretty much the story of my life back here in 1924.

"I have some other news," I said.

"Is it about that middle-aged black woman that Seamus saw beating rugs on the side porch of your property?"

"Actually, it is," I said.

I don't know why I thought anything could stay a secret longer than a minute in this town. Especially from Mary.

"I've hired Ruby and her husband to—"

"Seamus said he thought the man was missing his arms. I told him he needed to get his eyes tested because surely you wouldn't hire an armless black man to work your property."

"He's only missing one arm," I said.

She threw up her hands in bewilderment.

"Georgia, honestly! What are you thinking? Where will they live? Don't tell me they're living with you in the house?"

"Mary, you know perfectly well they are. When you interviewed for my staff didn't you advertise it as a live-in position?"

She huffed.

"Do they at least have references?"

"Neither of them has done this kind of work before so they have no references," I said. "But they're both hard-working very nice people."

"Until they rob you blind," she said.

"I'm more thinking they'll just collect the mail and cook and walk the dog, just like you said."

"I don't mind walking the dog!"

"Do me a favor and come visit while I'm gone—"

"—to keep an eye on them. I certainly will," she said.

"I was going to say to give Ruby some of Cook's recipes and maybe tell her husband Bert about the various hardware stores in the neighborhood. Also, if he needs any supplies, he knows to put it on my account at the hardware store. But I'll need you to step in if there's any trouble with that." I reached over to take her hand. "Mary, it's going to be fine. I have nothing to steal anyway."

"Are you sure you must go, Georgia? You've been through so much recently."

I squeezed her hand and then turned to feed a piece of chicken to Libby.

"You know I need to go. I've already missed the funeral. I need to settle things there."

"I worry about you."

"I know you do, dear friend. But it's going to be fine."

"Have you said goodbye to Jim?"

"In a manner of speaking."

"Uh oh. What does that mean?"

"I told him that I can travel to the future."

"Oh dear."

"I know. I'm not sure how he took it."

"How did he react?"

"He put on his pants and left."

"Georgia!" Mary said in mock horror and then we both began to laugh.

After we'd composed ourselves, she was the one to reach out to take my hand.

"Just be careful," she said. "And come back safe to us."

I squeezed her hand again.

"I have every intention of doing exactly that."

~

That night I sat on the back steps and watched the late evening sun dip below the horizon, casting my pretty garden into thick shadow. As I sat there breathing in the heady scents that hung in the humid air, I could almost see the blooms that perfumed the area. But even without seeing them, I knew where the trumpet vines were spilling wisteria blossoms in draping purple cascades on the back fence and also where the honeysuckle rambled over the arched trellises.

I smiled as I remembered how Mary had wanted me to have the honeysuckle dug up as an invasive pest, but I insisted on keeping it. And now it twisted up the porch columns in front too, its sweet nectar welcoming me home along with the heady jasmine that threaded through the picket fence. All in all, I'd finally decided that this townhouse and this time in Savannah was home for me. I knew I was taking a risk going back to 2024—both in aging and in my ability to return—something I never completely took for granted. But I needed to arrange for my mother's final resting place. I needed to go back and forgive myself for not being there when she passed. I couldn't do that here in a time before her birth.

I was just about to stand up to go to the spot in the garden from which I liked to leave when I noticed that one section of the shadowed garden was moving. It could've been a neighbor's cat except it was too big for that. A part of me knew I could just call out and Bert would be here in a flash with a bat or a kitchen butcher knife. But before I sucked in the breath to do that, Jim materialized out of his hiding spot.

"Well, this is a dramatic entrance," I said, willing my heartbeat to slow to a normal cadence. "You could've used the front door."

He walked over to me and then stopped when he saw how I was dressed. I had on a pair of skinny jeans, sneakers and a sweatshirt. There was nothing even remotely comparable to this outfit for women in 1924.

He came over to where I stood and sat down on the back porch step. He smelled nice. He smelled like cedar shavings and soap. Ever since our one night together, something seemed to have changed in how I felt about him. I now thought about him not as just a friend. I thought about him and wondered what he was doing. I wondered what he thought of me now. I wondered if I would ever see him again.

"So you're leaving tonight?" he asked.

"I have some things I have to do," I said. "Back there."

"In the future."

I wasn't sure where this conversation was going. I knew Jim must be still trying to process what I'd told him last night. I wasn't a hundred percent sure he didn't have a psychiatrist waiting in the bushes with asylum committal papers for me.

"In 2024," I said finally. "Yes."

We didn't speak for a moment. I honestly felt that the ball was in his court. If he couldn't deal with what I'd told him—or couldn't believe it—I'd totally understand. But it wasn't for me to pretend that nothing had happened.

"Are you coming back?"

"I'm going to try," I said. "It's not ever really a certain thing."

"I hope you do. I know this time probably doesn't have all the things that your time does…"

I turned on the steps and examined his face in near awe.

"I can't believe how easily you've accepted what I told you," I said in amazement.

"Well, I have to say that that laser leveler now makes a whole lot more sense."

I grinned and shook my head in disbelief.

"But still," I said. "Mary nearly had a nervous breakdown when I told her."

His eyebrows shot up in surprise.

"Mary knows? Does Sam?" Instantly Jim shook his head. "Of course not."

"No. You are in a very exclusive club, my dear."

He stood and drew me to him with his one good arm.

"I'd like it to stay that way," he said and kissed me softly, hungrily, thoroughly.

When the kiss ended, I found myself breathless and tingling all over. And not at all eager to move out of his embrace.

"If you're trying to convince me to come back," I said, my eyes glistening as I looked into his, "you're doing a crackerjack job."

"Come back to me," he said.

"I will," I said, looking at him sadly. "If I can."

ABOUT THE AUTHOR

USA TODAY Bestselling Author Susan Kiernan-Lewis is the author of *The Maggie Newberry Mysteries,* the post-apocalyptic thriller series *The Irish End Games, The Mia Kazmaroff Mysteries, The Stranded in Provence Mysteries, The Claire Baskerville Mysteries,* and *The Savannah Time Travel Mysteries.*

Visit her website at www.susankiernanlewis.com or follow her at Author Susan Kiernan-Lewis on Facebook.

∽

Books by Susan Kiernan-Lewis
The Maggie Newberry Mysteries
Murder in the South of France
Murder à la Carte
Murder in Provence
Murder in Paris
Murder in Aix
Murder in Nice
Murder in the Latin Quarter

Murder in the Abbey
Murder in the Bistro
Murder in Cannes
Murder in Grenoble
Murder in the Vineyard
Murder in Arles
Murder in Marseille
Murder in St-Rémy
Murder à la Mode
Murder in Avignon
Murder in the Lavender
Murder in Mont St-Michel
Murder in the Village
Murder in St-Tropez
Murder in Grasse
Murder in Monaco
Murder in the Villa
Murder in Montmartre
Murder in Toulouse
A Provençal Christmas: A Short Story
A Thanksgiving in Provence
Laurent's Kitchen

The Claire Baskerville Mysteries
Déjà Dead
Death by Cliché
Dying to be French
Ménage à Murder
Killing it in Paris
Murder Flambé
Deadly Faux Pas
Toujours Dead
Murder in the Christmas Market

Deadly Adieu
Murdering Madeleine
Murder Carte Blanche
Death à la Drumstick
Murder Mon Amour

The Savannah Time Travel Mysteries
Killing Time in Georgia
Scarlett Must Die
The Cottonmouth Club

The Stranded in Provence Mysteries
Parlez-Vous Murder?
Crime and Croissants
Accent on Murder
A Bad Éclair Day
Croak, Monsieur!
Death du Jour
Murder Très Gauche
Wined and Died
Murder, Voila!
A French Country Christmas
Fromage to Eternity
Crepe Expectations

The Irish End Games
Free Falling
Going Gone
Heading Home
Blind Sided
Rising Tides
Cold Comfort
Never Never

Wit's End
Dead On
White Out
Black Out
End Game

The Mia Kazmaroff Mysteries
Reckless
Shameless
Breathless
Heartless
Clueless
Ruthless

Ella Out of Time
Swept Away
Carried Away
Stolen Away